Since his tragic death, H. Beam Piper has become one of the most popular names in science fiction. Ace is delighted to have been able to republish Piper's hard-to-find short stories, in the collections called *Federation, Empire,* and *Paratime.* Now you hold in your hands another treat for Piper fans: a *lost novel.*

The manuscript for *First Cycle* was discovered among Piper's papers, along with extensive notes. The novel was complete; all that remained was the fleshing-out and polishing process that would ready it for publication. Michael Kurland, working from Piper's manuscript and notes, has taken on that task, expanding *First Cycle* into a novel that we believe Piper himself would have been proud of.

Here, then, a *new* novel by H. Beam Piper

FIRST CYCLE
EDITED & EXPANDED BY
MICHAEL KURLAND

Other titles of interest from Ace Science Fiction:

A NOVEL BY

H. BEAM PIPER

FIRST
CYCLE

EDITED & EXPANDED BY

MICHAEL KURLAND

SF
ace books
A Division of Charter Communications Inc.
A GROSSET & DUNLAP COMPANY
51 Madison Avenue
New York, New York 10010

FIRST CYCLE
copyright © 1982 by Charter Communications, Inc.

An ACE Book

First Ace printing: January 1982
Published Simultaneously in Canada

2 4 6 8 0 9 7 5 3 1
Manufactured in the United States of America

Chapter One

For endless millenia the red dwarf, pulled from its home orbit by some random stellar happenstance, crossed the lonely void between the two galaxies of the near universe. Curving and twisting through the competing attraction—weak but inevitable—of the gravity wells of distant nebulae, it gradually swung around to head toward a particular medium-sized star cluster. Penetrating the cluster, it bore straight toward the eight-planet system of a yellow-white star thirty-eight light years from the cluster's gravitic center.

The eighth planet, and the seventh, and the sixth, were on the far sides of their orbits as the red dwarf approached; but the fifth, a methane giant with three major satellites, was in harm's way. As they closed together, the planet heated; its coating of frigid gasses flowed, and then vaporized. Great tidal forces tore at the planet's dense, solid core. Quakes and explosions shook the surface; the atmosphere burned.

For an instant, during which the great planet seemed to hesitate in its orbit, the seismic insult increased past endurance. Two of the three major

1

moons were ripped away; they spiraled inward to the yellow star and disappeared as though they had never been. The third satellite, torn almost equally between its mother planet and the passing dwarf, slowed in its orbit, and then, as the red star passed, came crashing down on its primary. This final shock broke the giant planet into two almost equal halves, and a minor planet's worth of solar debris.

The red dwarf, dragging the broken halves after it, dived toward the yellow star. The fourth planet escaped with no more than superficial damage, the third passed unscathed. But the second was directly in the path of the destroyer. It swung from its orbit, spun madly for an instant, and then hurtled into the red star like a racing scull ramming a battleship.

Relatively, the planet's mass and impact were trivial; the sacrificial collision, however, prevented a greater catastrophe at the center of the system. The invader caromed slightly off course, lost momentum, and was trapped. The attraction of the yellow sun, the lesser attractions of the planet family, and the red dwarf's own new velocity combined to pin it to an orbit slightly greater than that of the planet it had just annihilated. Spinning around one another like a pair of bar-shot on an ever-shortening bar, the two fragments of the fifth planet followed it.

In time, as time is measured in the cosmos, the system stabilized. The frozen outer planets wheeled around their ancient orbits. The shattered fifth had left a wide gap. There was a thin belt of meteoric debris inside the orbit of the third. And, just beyond the orbit of the vanished second, the newcomer and her own new satellite chain traced and re-traced the orbits imposed on them; yellow star, red dwarf, and attendant fragments forming a three-body system at the apexes of a one-hundred and fifty million kilometer equilateral triangle.

The two planet fragments slowly accommodated themselves to one another and to the rest of their violently re-formed solar system. They crumbled, pulled together, compressed into spheres. Stripped of all atmosphere in the cataclysm which had sundered them, they formed now gaseous envelopes, lost them as the heated gas molecules escaped, formed other atmospheres, and held them as their surfaces cooled. At first they rotated on their own axes as they revolved around a common center of gravity. As they drew closer together, this axial rotation slowed until, at a quarter-million kilometers, they faced each other as though on opposite sides of a merry-go-round mounted on the rim of a gigantic Ferris-wheel, each slightly bulging toward the other. At the center of their inner, or opposing, hemispheres, high mountains had pushed outward, surrounded by concentric ranges of lower mountains raised by the tilt of the rock strata, sloping back into wide plains which extended to the terminator-zones, which were jumbled badlands of great, shattered boulders. On each, at the point antipodal to the other, the crust had sunk into a deep depression, around which chains of great mountains had been formed.

In the early stages of their formation, one of this pair had received most of the water available. Thus it differed from its twin in that it was covered by a vast ocean, broken only by the tops of the mountain chain around the central depression on the outer hemisphere, which formed a circle of small island continents, the largest about three million square kilometers in area. The inner hemisphere, the side always facing the twin, had a permanent high tide, which just covered the top of the great peak at the center.

On the sister planet, the central depression of the outer hemisphere was a shallow, brackish sea; there was a chain of lakes and marshes encircling the terminator or Horizon Zone, and another circle of lakes around the central peaks of the inner hemisphere.

On both planets life emerged, quickly on the water world, more slowly on the arid one. Seaweed sprang up from the marshes, wind and spray borne spores invaded the land, and the green of plant life spread over the mineral reds and yellows and browns and grays. Animal life followed. The world-ocean of the water planet sent wave after wave of invaders ashore—sea-worms which evolved into earthworms, mollusks, crustaceans, and then a vertebrate fish which developed the ability to breathe air and became an amphibian. On the arid planet, vertebrate life never developed in the central sea; but a crawling slugoid, twenty-five centimeters long, which had invaded the land, developed some of its muscles into cartilage. After another million years, the cartilage hardened to bone.

With some superficial modification, this was the situation on the twin planets when, in the 572nd year of the Primary Dispersion, the Greater Terran

Federation space-cruiser *Franklin,* G.T.F.H.
17649, Captain Absalom Carpenter, came out of
hyperspace at the perimeter of the Canis Venatici
star-cluster and picked up the binary system on her
scanners.

By custom, commanders of G.T.F. Space Navy
Exploration and Discovery vessels named newly
discovered planetary systems either for themselves
or for their ships, mistresses, wives, or pet dogs.
Absalom Carpenter, G.T.F.S.N.E.&.D. Captain,
Commanding, was, however, an odd number even
in a service not noted for robot-like conformity.
The breast of his dress tunic was polychromatic
with decoration and campaign and battle ribbons,
but he valued them, even the blue one with the
silver stars, far less than the single Lit. D. which
the University of Montevideo had awarded him for
his *Internal Clues to the Probable Dates and Identi-
ties of the Secondary and Tertiary Authors of the
Iliad and the Odyssey.* So, following some private
association-path through the legends of ancient
Hellas, he named the yellow star Elektra. The red
dwarf, obviously, was named Rubra, and he called
the watery planet on which the expedition first
landed Thalassa, and its arid companion Hetaira.

Chapter Two

By the end of the first billion years, the coastal marshes of Equatorial Thalassa teemed with life. Pools and channels were clogged with water-grasses and water-ferns. Great banyan-like trees dipped their branches, sending out new roots to gain additional resistance to storms and floods. Fish-like and worm-like and snake-like things swarmed the waters; beasts ran and crawled on the silted floors, or flew or scampered among the branches.

Twice a year the sun would stand at zenith as it spiralled back and forth around the planet, briefly parching the treetops and driving the flying and scampering beasts down into the lower shadows. The winds would follow, with violent storms of lightning and down-sheeting rain; the rivers would rise, spreading over the whole jungle and driving the creatures of the ground up into the trees. Sometimes whole islands would disintegrate, and matted masses of trees would be swept out to sea. Then the storms would end; the air would grow colder; often there would be thin skims of ice on the ponds, and sometimes a few flakes of snow would sift down through the leaf-roof above. And then the air would warm again, there would be fresh vegetation on the flats where the silt had caught, and the jungles would vibrate with life again.

Eventually a small, mammal-like creature made its appearance among these swamps and jungles, living in the trees, sometimes dropping to the ground in search of food. It had four limbs, each terminating in handlike members with four fingers and two opposing thumbs. Its head was almost spherical, a little lopsided at the bottom from heavy jaws. It would eat almost anything—fruit, nuts, grubs, fish, smaller animals, leathery reptile eggs dug out of the mud, and mollusks which it would break out of their shells. At first it used its teeth for this, later it learned to lay the shellfish on a stone and hammer it open with another stone. It learned to use stones to break through the ice in cold weather to catch fish, and to throw when attacked. Eventually it learned to carry quite large stones into the trees and cache them in crotches to drop on larger animals.

The changes of temperature forced it to develop an efficient internal cooling system, and, in addition, its body was covered with a soft down, really microscopic feathers. During the hot season it would moult it away and sweat copiously; as the temperature dropped the down would grow out again. The creature built nests in the trees, lining them with soft grasses and with its own down.

As generations passed, it spent more and more of its time on the ground, taking to the trees only to escape the floods or dangerous carnivores; and its physical structure became more and more adapted to life out of the trees. It developed stronger muscles in its rear limbs, and came to rely upon them alone for locomotion, using the hands of its forelimbs for food-gathering. Its posture became more erect; its body grew larger, until, where its little arboreal ancestor had massed eight to ten kilograms, the average mass was now around eighty kilos. It was still covered with greenish down, but it shed it more readily and grew it only in the coldest weather. Its legs became short and sturdy, its arms long. Its hands were well adapted to grasping and manipulating; its feet broad and webbed between the toes to give support in the soft mud and speed in the water.

Like its ancestors, it still built tree-nests, in which it slept. The chance cobbles which its ancestors had used for missiles or hammers no longer satisfied it; it chose stones discriminatingly and improved them by chipping. It manufactured hand-choppers and flake knives. It gained ability to control and produce fire, and, most important of all, it learned to communicate with its fellows by oral sounds which gradually acquired specific informational values and became words.

Among the ponds and salt-marshes of Hetaira's Horizon Zone another small animal looked up to face a mighty destiny. Its immediate ancestor had been a lizard-like rock-dweller which had enjoyed a brief prosperity when, as a result of a complex chain of ecological events, an order of beetle-like insects on which it had fed had suddenly multiplied in numbers. The increased food supply had caused an explosion in the population of the rock-dwellers, which resulted in the rapid over-hunting and extermination of the food-insect. Facing a hungry future, the rock-dwellers were forced into readjustments. Some specialized themselves for feeding on another type of insect, developing a long snout and a beautifully efficient digging-paw. Some took to robbing the nests of an oviparous pterodactyl-thing among the high rocks. And some moved up into the woods above the marshes.

Gradually, over hundreds of thousands of years, the progeny of these last developed binocular vision and forepaws with digits—four fingers of unequal length and a thick, short, opposing thumb. Their bodies were covered with bright red fur; they looked, more than anything else, like cats with the limbs of monkeys. They would eat anything, animal or vegetable. They learned to use sticks for digging out roots and knocking down fruit. They would use long whip-like withes to kill low flying bat-birds and small animals. A couple of them wielding the long withes could even discourage attacks by fairly large animals. When cornered, they were vicious fighters, with nails and teeth but to escape the larger carnivora they relied chiefly upon agility, and developed longer legs for running and jumping, proportionally smaller torsos, and arms and hands more and more specialized for gathering food.

They were incredibly lecherous beasts; the males chased not only the females of their own species, but of any other even remotely similar. On some of these, not too distantly related, they begot hybrids which occasionally bred true and formed new subspecies; but the real importance of this sexual cath-

olicity was the competitive development of sex-at-
traction characteristics among their own females.
Instead of passively awaiting the male, the female
sought him out and flaunted her charms before
him. Mating, among these monkey-cats of Hetaira,
was not a matter of coy seduction—it was a head-
on collision.

This pattern led to a certain tolerance and
absence of jealousy among the males; each was
quite willing to share his plural mates with another.
Instead of the family, the social unit became the
gang—a dozen or so males and females, the sex ra-
tio changing with circumstance, and the randomly-
begotten offspring cared for by all.

Such a gang was more than a match for any of
the carnivora of Hetaira, and could pull down and
kill any but the very largest herbivores. They
learned to use stones for hammers and choppers
and hand-weapons and missiles; they invented innumerable tricks of cooperative hunting and fighting, and since cooperation demands communication, they slowly developed the rudiments of
speech. They made themselves feared; at the approach of one of their gangs, big meat-eaters that
had hitherto been kings of the forest learned to
slink away, or they did not live to learn.

So, when one such gang of red-furred scam-
perers rounded a bend in a game-trail and found
themselves confronted by a big pink-and-maroon
striped thing with vermillion jowl-tufts like Lord
Dundreary whiskers and a single sabre-fang at the
apex of a V-shaped jaw, one of them picked up a
stone and threw it, hitting the tiger-thing in the
face. Instead of fleeing, the beast roared in fury and

charged. The gang scattered quickly out of the way. The one directly in front of the animal jumped behind a small bush, pulled it down, waited for an instant, and then released it. The bush lashed forward into the beast's face. Another snatched a ten-foot length of dead branch and shoved it between the animal's front legs. Three more jumped in to catch hold of the tiger-thing's tail; the others swarmed over it with stones and clubs. There was a brief howling, writhing convulsion in the brush, and then the one who had released the bush in the beast's face jumped in with a heavy stone raised in its two hands, and smashed in the thing's head. The others stoned it frantically while it twitched on the ground, and kept stoning it for quite a while after it had stopped twitching. Gradually they realized that the thing was really dead, and the stoning died off and stopped.

Then they saw that their victory had come at a price. One of the females, who had rushed in with a sharp stick when the others had caught the beast's tail, had been ripped from throat to belly by the back-raking claws. The gang stood looking at her for a while, and then first one, then another of them turned and began tearing gobbets of meat from the dead tiger-thing and stuffing them into their mouths.

All but one male, whose favorite mate she had been. He remained crouching beside her, clumsily trying to rearrange the mangled viscera, to close the wound, to somehow arouse her from her endless sleep. Some of the others left the feast to join him. One of the females, still chewing on a piece of tiger-thing flank, put a furry arm over his furry shoulder and tried to comfort him. Tearing the meat with her teeth, she offered him half of it. He sank his teeth into the bloody gobbet and chewed, at first mechanically and then with relish. When they finally left the dead female beside the striped body of the beast, he was chewing on a bone and walking beside the female who had comforted him. As he walked the memory of his dead mate began to fade. He liked this female too, and his was not a level of mental activity capable of much projection beyond the immediate.

But somewhere in the back of his mind there smouldered a murderous hatred for the big striped tiger-things. The next time he encountered one, after some twenty sleeps—each of which might have been anywhere from six to twelve hours, broken by waking periods of fifteen to thirty—he snatched up stones and began hurling them rapidly and accurately, gibbering in fury. The maroon-striped, Dundreary-whiskered monster snorted in surprise and fled.

Everything fled or fell before the roving gangs. The whole forest was their playground; they hunted and fed and romped through it for millennia. They might have stopped there, satisfied with the niche they had carved out for themselves, but for one thing. These little red-furred gangsters had begun to think, and to question, and to imagine.

Chapter Three

Upon Thalassa, too, the sun still spiralled up to zenith and back again; the seasons changed and recurred. Forests invaded open grasslands, and grasslands spread after retreating forests. Families and bands of families left the swamp and wandered into the uplands; sometimes other groups, trusting to the protection of their tree-nests, were swept out to sea in the biennial floods, occasionally to survive as castaways upon other shores. Race after race of these primordial humanoids appeared, wandered, vanished, left their scattered monuments of chipped stone weapons and fire-blackened caves and kitchen-middens.

On the large, roughly triangular continent which would someday be called Gvarda, a race finally appeared which had reached that point in the journey of physical evolution where they were ready to proceed from rudimentary socialization to true cultural advancement. They were short and stocky, but their feet were narrower and less pronouncedly webbed, and they could use their two-thumbed hands with equal facility in either direction and possessed considerable flexibility in the elbow-joint. The body down had completely disappeared from their green-gray skins; there was still down on their heads, blue-green to green in color. They had large eyes, wide, jutting noses, heavy prognathous jaws, and pointed ears that could be moved independently.

The tree-nests of their ancestors had become tree-houses, flexibly but strongly built to withstand the high winds following the hot seasons. They had learned to twist ropes of bark-fiber and plant-fiber and rawhide and animal-gut, and to make cunning knots and lashings. They chipped stone expertly, making hafted axes and hammers from the cores, and knives and awls and spear-points from the flakes. They designed a wide variety of bone-tipped fish-spears. They learned to hollow out pirogues from logs, with fire and the stone adze. They wove baskets, and made garments of downy skins.

They called themselves the Navva. As with primitive peoples everywhere, this simply meant "The People."

At times, after the floods, small parties would go up the river in pirogues, to where the more open forests of the uplands began. Such parties would camp and then divide up to hunt and smoke meat, and quarry and chip stone, returning to the delta country before the next flood season with their spoils. Sometimes they would return again and again, bringing their families. Some groups decided to stay, building their tree-houses high and taking chances with the floods. And so permanent villages began to appear along the tributary streams of the big river.

The pirogues which had served so well in the

coastal swamps were too clumsy for the smaller streams and too heavy to carry over frequent portages. Some of the upland forests were too open for building tree-houses, but there was no need for them on ground always above flood-level. A house on the ground could be built strong enough to resist all but the largest animals—and those were all herbivores. So they began to build huts of poles and bark, and fence them with pole stockades interwoven with thornbrush. They used their basket-weaving skills to construct lighter boats, covering them with skins treated with animal fats and tree-resins. And, while bending split wood for boat-frames, they invented the bow.

With these new skills in transportation and defense and hunting, they spread through the uplands, increasing in numbers as more of their young survived to reach maturity. Stockaded forest villages appeared at portage-places and the juncture of streams. Canoes and parties on foot pressed up the rivers and along the game-trails. These people no longer called themselves simply "the Navva." They were "Navvadrov," the Forest People, to distinguish themselves from "Navva-zorf," the Swamp People.

Crossing mountain after mountain, they came at last to the High Ridge, with its drop in three bench-like stages to the plains two kilometers below. Here they found the blue-black Wahanavva, the Not-People. Survivors of one of the races of the past, these were cave-dwellers who had progressed no further than fire and crudely chipped stone hand-axes. At first, when they came swarming out of the rocks to attack, they were feared. When it was seen that they would just mill around stupidly while they were shot down with arrows, they came to be despised. But it was generations before they were exterminated and the Navvadrov could descend from the High Ridge into the open veldt beyond.

In the swamps, the Navvazorf had begun building their houses on piles, independent of the trees. They constructed silt-traps and levees of earth packed between woven brush fences, and thus filled in selected areas of the swamps. The mud-flats widened, and on them were planted the wild grasses whose seeds they ground into flour, and tubers to roast along with their fish and meat. They found fruit trees and tended them and learned to prune them. Weapons and boats and fishing-tackle improved; the bark fibers of which they made ropes were woven into mats, and then cloth.

Hunting parties still went up the river; there they met and traded with their cousins the Navvadrov, bringing home the bow and the art of making pots from baked clay. In return the Navvadrov received skin bags of flour, and dried fish, and shell, and mats, and cloth. The Navvadrov themselves had made something of a beginning at agriculture; they cultivated certain plants to attract game to their area, and soon progressed from this to planting food-crops for themselves. After observing the effects of a few accidental fires on the wild grasslands, they learned to use fire as a tool to clear land for planting.

The introduction of pottery among the Navvazorf further speeded the progress of both peoples. Jars of fish-oil and fermented grain beverages went up the river, along with flour, grain, dried

fish, and cloth, to be exchanged for flint and obsidian and animal-skins. A regular trading-place
came into being on the flat river-beach at the
mouth of one of the larger tributaries; from a temporary camp it became a permanent village. Navvadrov families settled there, hunting and farming
between visits of the down-river traders. Long
sheds were erected to house trade-goods, storage
paid for in kind. Bows and arrows were made
there; traded skins were sewn into robes, and stone
tools were finished and set and reset into wooden
handles. The place came to be called Amarush—
literally, Where We Sit and Barter.

Among the people of the coastal swamps, a sort
of democratic socialism prevailed. Crops were
planted and harvested in common, each family
being responsible for its fair share of the work.
Catches of fish were smoked and stored as common stock. The business of the villages was conducted in open conclave of all adult males who had
"Walked the Walk," as the rite of passage for
males was called. The women and children yelled
assent or disapproval from the sidelines. So, when
the trade with the people up the Gvaru became important, each Navvazorf village selected a family to
move up to Amarush and deal with the uplanders.

Tammak, chief of the Darbba, sat on his pile of
skin robes at the end of the village council-hut and
looked across the fire at the dozen-odd tribal elders
who had gathered with him. His throat was dry,
and his hands clenched on the rawhide-wrapped
grip of the stone mace that was both his personal
weapon and his scepter of status. It was now, he
realized, or never. The thing he was about to pro-

pose was frighteningly novel, and novelty, at best, was always frightening. A chieftain ruled only as far, and as long, as his people were willing to accept his rule, and this thing he had dreamed of would be hard for them to accept, or even comprehend.

"It is still two sun-trips until the hot season, and the trading will not start for another sun-trip after that," one of the elders said. "Why need we hurry? The longer we wait, the more skins we will have to trade."

"We will not take skins to trade," Tammak explained. "We will take only our weapons. The women and children, who will follow behind us, will carry the skins along with the rest of the household goods."

"But we cannot trade our weapons!" an elder objected. "And why must the women and children come? That has never been heard of. Trading journeys are for men!"

"It is so," Tammak agreed. "But we will not trade. We will go early to Amarush, before any of the trading groups arrive, and we will kill everybody in the village and take it for ourselves."

"A raid? A raid on Amarush? That has never been heard of. No one raids Amarush. Amarush is the place where we barter."

"And why are we to take our women and children on a raid? That has never been heard of. Let them wait here, where they will be safe!"

"It is not to be a raid. It is to be something-greater-than-a-raid, and we will not return. We will stay forever in Amarush."

"But our fields are here! And our village! Tammak, the gods have been spitting on you! The job of our chief is to lead us in defense of our fields and our village, not to lead us away from them!"

"Amarush is a better village than this, and there are good fields at Amarush. We will take Amarush, and trade with the people from down-river who come to Amarush, and the people from the woods, and the mountains. I have seen the traders of Amarush. They live in fine houses, much better than our poor huts. They have garments of thin cloth for the summers and of soft-downed skins and thick quilted cloth for the winters. They sit in the shade of their awnings; they feast, wasting enough food at a meal to feed two families. Why should we not take what they have and live easily, as they do?"

"But that is not proper, Tammak," one of the elders cried out. Gozzom, who was next eldest to Tammak, and by tribal custom his successor. Tammak shifted his grip slightly on the mace-handle. "We are not traders," Gozzom continued, "we are hunters and farmers. Our fathers were hunters and farmers, and our children will be hunters and farmers. It is what the gods have chosen for us; it is what the gods expect of us. It is not right for people who are one thing to try to be something else. It goes against the gods."

Tammak jumped to his feet, whirling his mace around his head, and smashed it down on Gozzom's skull. The bone crushed like eggshell, and blood and bits of brain splattered the mace and Tammak's arm and chest. Gozzom fell.

Tammak stood up straight. He pointed with the blood-splattered mace at Gozzom's body. "Look at that thing," he said as calmly as his heavy breathing would allow. The others stared at the lifeless lump that had been Gozzom, shock and amazement showing on their faces.

"A thing that was once a living man is now something else. And the gods do not speak! Is there anyone else in this circle who needs to be shown that it is possible to change from one thing to another?"

The elders shifted uncomfortably, but none of them spoke. Together they could have torn him to pieces, and they probably would have liked to at that moment, but the first one would have died in the attempt. None of them wished to be that sacrificial first.

"It is a hard life to be hunters and farmers," Tammak said. "We can be rich and well-fed at Amarush. I have given this much thought over many sleeps. We will take a part of everything that is brought there. We will no longer wear dirty skins. Our children will no longer be naked and hungry—"

There was less trouble with the rest of the tribe. Some of the women made a fearful outcry against leaving familiar homes for a trek into the unknown, but they were only women; the men let them squall or cuffed them into silence. They were soon too busy at the work of constructing the needed new canoes. The younger tribesmen were, without exception, enthusiastic.

When they were ready to start, Tammak had every hut in the village fired, and they paddled downstream with their village burning behind them. Now the Darbba must go on; they had nothing to return to.

It took almost a sun-trip to reach Amarush on the big river. There could, of course, be no night attack on this world of forever-daylight, and as a precaution against raids or forest-fires, the trees had been cleared for two bow-shots around Amarush. But Tammak had given this much thought. The best concealment, he had decided, would be the most open approach. Bundles stuffed with leaves were made of all the sleeping-robes. Chunks of stone were slung on poles and carried between two men. The larger pots and jars were suspended from shoulder-yokes, as though they contained lard or honey. Shouting and singing, the males of the Darbba marched across the cleared ground toward the barter-place at Amarush.

It was early, before the usual beginning of trading. The merchants of Amarush, expecting good bargains in the bundles and pots of these first-comers, flocked out to greet them. Almost all of the merchants were in the market-place when the Darbba flung aside their burdens, snatched up their weapons and set upon them. Within thirty minutes, Amarush and all it contained had fallen to the invaders.

It was then that Tammak showed the wisdom he had gained his years as chief. The houses of the Navvazorf trading representatives were left unmolested. There was no burning or indiscriminate looting. Women and children were spared and adopted into the Darbba tribe, as were the old skilled bowyers, fletchers, flint-knappers and other artisans who had stayed behind in the village. Knowing that what could be done once would probably be attempted again, Tammak immediately put everyone to work constructing a heavy pole stockade all around the village. His people and the Navvazorf traders lived inside the stockade; the trading was carried on at picked places around the outside. Between trading seasons the women cultivated crops and dressed skins, the men hunted and fished, and made tools and weapons.

The Darbba waxed rich after the conquest of Amarush. Tammak bought the products of both the coast and the uplands, and he allowed no trading in Amarush except through his own people. There was a wide variety of merchandise—wine and fish-oil and dried fruits and smoked fish and nuts and nut-oil, rough and shaped flint and quartz and obsidian, skins and baskets and mats and cloth. From the farther uplands a new trade-stone was beginning to trickle in—small pebbles of a soft, shining yellow stuff which could be pounded into sheets and drawn into wire as no stone could be, and which would, when heated in the hottest part of a charcoal fire, flow like melted tallow.

A large nugget of this stuff was among the loot which fell into Tammak's hands at the taking of Amarush. Laying it on a smooth rock, he beat it with a polished flint hammer, intending to make a cup or bowl of it. However, before he had mastered the technique he had pounded the yellow stuff too thin, so he shaped it into a rough cone. His woman lined it with a cap of downy skin, and Tammak wore it on his head. Years later, when he knew he was going to die, he gave it, and the rule of Amarush, to his eldest son, Vallak.

So Tammak I of Amarush was the first of the kings of Thalassa to wear a golden crown, and it was he who established the principle of royal succession by primogeniture.

Chapter Four

Generation after generation of the red-furred gangsters of Hetaira scampered among the forests, valleys and lakes of the Horizon Zone. The sounds by which they communicated with one another became more varied, the expressed meanings more exact. Their tools and weapons of stone underwent constant improvement, first discarded after use and then retained against future need. The gangs grew larger; splitting when hunting was poor, reuniting and merging in times of plenty. They raided each others' territory, tried to kidnap or entice each others' females, fought and made friends.

With each advance life became easier. More individuals survived to maturity; pregnant and nursing mothers, and growing young, were better and better nourished; each generation showed the effect. They grew taller, legs lengthening as their posture altered; shoulders widened and hips narrowed. The head became larger with increased brain capacity; the jaws lighter and narrower as the teeth ceased to be used for anything but chewing food. Because the females bore young at fairly long intervals, and because the young were, almost without exception, single births and very small at birth, pregnancy and childbirth were negligible hardships, never curtailing other activity. There was little difference between the sexes in strength and endurance, hence the division of labor within the gang was by age and status rather than sex, and the race began its upward journey on a basis of sexual equality.

Over the centuries their artifacts were refined into greater efficiency. Delicately chipped hafted axes appeared, and flake knives with rawhide-wrapped grips, and spears with needle-sharp flint core heads. Fire early became their servant. They made garments of skins, and belts and pouches and packs to carry their multiplying possessions. A fire carrier—the skull of a large animal lined with clay and slung from a rawhide strap—was invented; and from this beginning, pottery was developed. The immemorial trick of springing branches or brush in the face of a pursuer suggested the sling, and eventually the bow. Hetaira was a world without feathers, as Thalassa was a hairless world, but there were stiff broad-bladed grasses which, when dried and split, made excellent vanes for arrows. They learned to make spear-throwers too, and bolas of rawhide rope weighted with round stones.

These little red gangsters had a vast curiosity about everything, a hunger to know and understand. Unless some immediate cause of hostility existed, gangs of strangers would meet and squat in a circle, exchanging information. They tested everything they found by smelling and tasting and pounding and cutting and burning. They practiced unthinking cruelties of investigation on every living thing they caught. They learned, sometimes by trial and error, and sometimes by accident. But once they had learned, they never forgot.

There was, for example, the contribution to gangster knowledge which cost Nwilt his life.

Nwilt had been squatting patiently, motionlessly, in the brush for almost an hour, his bow bent, waiting for the big blue-furred bat-bird to circle close enough for a shot. Finally the thing swooped within range, the bowstring twanged, and the bat-bird jerked convulsively and died, its wings extended. As it glided down, Nwilt jumped from his ambush and ran after it, coming to the edge of a pond in time to see it land fifty feet from the bank in the scum-covered water.

He growled in annoyance. This was one of the black-scum ponds his people ran across sometimes, its surface covered with a viscid stuff which had a nauseous smell and a worse taste. He looked at the bat-bird and wrinkled his nose in disgust. If he fished it out at once and washed it, it would be fit to eat. His gang had not done so well at hunting lately, and besides, one of his best arrows was sticking in the beast's side. He cut and trimmed a pole and, prodding it ahead of him, waded into the horrible stuff and recovered the bat-bird.

On the way back his foot slipped, and before he could right himself he had fallen sprawling. Picking himself up, he regained the bank, jabbering the inarticulate blasphemy of the godless and obscenity of the uninhibited, and set off toward the smoke-wisp that marked the gang's stopping-place. The air was cold—it was several sleep-periods since the sun had set, far to the north—and he was shivering from the ducking by the time he reached the fire, around which the twenty males and females and children of the gang were squatting.

In his absence someone had shot an animal, a medium sized thing like an antelope, with a single horn projecting straight forward from above and between its eyes. The blood-wet skin was draped over a bush; one of the gang had broken the horn out of the skull to fashion a dagger, and the unicorn, already gutted, was turning on a spit over the fire. Nwilt flung down his bedraggled trophy and crowded up to the fire to warm himself.

He crowded too close. A moment later he was wrapped in flames, screaming in agony, and running frantically about. One of the others tangled his legs with a bolas and brought him down; in a second the whole gang was swarming over him with sleeping-robes, the wet unicorn-skin, the water pot. They got the fire out, but too late to help Nwilt, who was already dead.

The whole gang was considerably shocked by the incident. Not at the death of Nwilt; death was an old story and a constant companion to them. For for a person to burst into flames like a pitch-soaked faggot, that was frightening. It might happen without warning to any of them.

"We might have all caught fire from him," a woman said, "just as sticks catch fire from a burning stick." She rubbed a handful of mud on a spot where her fur was scorched.

"We didn't have time to think of that," a man said. "Besides, people don't just catch fire. If you get too close to the fire, you might get burned, but you won't burst into flames."

"*He* did," one of the women pointed out.

"I smelled black scum on him when he came up to the fire," another woman said. "I think he must have fallen into a scum-pond."

A man poked at the dead bat-bird with his spear point. "That thing is covered with black-scum," he said. "It was shot with an arrow. Maybe Nwilt shot it and it fell in a scum-pond, and he waded in after it." He gingerly picked up a burning brand from the fire, stepped back, and threw it on the bat-bird. "Let's see what happens now."

The bat-bird blazed up. When the fire went out, at last, it was badly charred.

"Well," one of the older men said. "It was the black-scum that caught fire. We must remember that."

An adolescent named Brilk looked at the body of Nwilt and then at the charred remains of the bat-bird. "If the black-scum makes people and bat-birds catch fire," he suggested, "maybe it makes other things catch fire. Maybe it would make wet wood catch fire."

The others turned and looked at him for a moment, and in that moment Brilk ceased to speak as a child and became one of the gang council.

"So it should, Brilk," one of the others agreed. "Let's try it."

The next time they met a strange gang, after they settled a hunting dispute and made ritualistic gestures toward stealing each others' women, they made the peace-sign, and both gangs squatted in a circle. The others listened intently while the gang reported the discovery of petroleum.

Then there was the time when a gang built a

campfire against an outcropping of bituminous coal. That was a frightening experience, too, until it was realized that coal was a special kind of rock. The idea that the very rock they walked on might catch fire from any campfire was frightening. But from understanding that coal was different, although it *looked* like rock, came the understanding that things that look alike are not necessarily the same, and that things might possess properties not evident from outside appearance.

The gangs drifted north and south through the Horizon Zone. Thousands of years passed until two gangs met, half way around the planet, and found that neither could understand the language of the other. At times, from mountain tops, they would glimpse a thing of beauty on the far horizon: a faintly luminous ball, larger than a man's fist at arm's length. Now and then a gang would move toward it, leaving the zone of jumbled mountains and reaching open plains beyond. Some followed the rivers that fed the lakes of the Horizon Zone until they found their way barred by deserts. Then they might wander back and forth until, by chance, they would find another river flowing in the opposite direction and follow it between ever higher mountain ranges until at last they came to another land of lakes, and of mountains higher than they had ever seen before, pushing their snow-capped peaks miles into the air. And, almost at the zenith, the silvery globe.

The beauty of that thing in the sky fascinated them as the sun and the Star-Cluster and Rubra never did. They never tired of watching it, and they felt somehow attracted to it. But they made no

myths about it; they did not worship it as a god.
They had no gods, and the very concept of a supreme being was incomprehensible to them. They
asked questions, and they accepted nothing on
faith. They asked: What is it? What holds it up?
How far away is it? What is it really like? They of
Hetaira had escaped the two blind alleys of religion
and magic; they had already learned that things of
nature had natural causes, and that if one were
smart enough to ask the proper questions, nature
would not withhold its secrets.

There were many gods upon Thalassa, and magic ruled the lives of its people. When Amarush was
still a huddle of temporary huts on a flat beach, a
thriving trade in magical articles existed—colored
or glittering stones, roots in animal or humanoid
form, seashells valued as fertility charms—and the
concept of pure magic had already become
elaborated into belief in some supernatural power
behind the magical influences.

The god of the Navvazorf was the sun. Of the
three major sky-objects, only Elektra gave heat as
well as light; it brought the storms and bloods, pro-
viding fresh silt to renew the land for planting. At
first it was worshipped directly, and then as the
god's abode, and finally as the god's visible man-
ifestation. Rubra and the Star-Cluster were also
venerated, but their cults gradually merged into the
worship of Dindash, the Sun God. Altars rose;
sacrifice-fires blazed; priests howled and chanted
as they moved from orgiastic dance to ceremonial
procession.

The Navvadrov, the Upland People, at first had

a complex system of animal-totems and ancestor spirit cults. The priest remained half wizard, purveying charms even as he offered prayers. When agriculture and the breeding of domestic animals began to supplant hunting, the deities of the Navvadrov became fertility gods; a polytheism arose, with Mother-Goddess, Father-God, slain and risen Seed-God, and a host of field-gods and herd-gods and local and special deities.

Those of the Navvadrov who had crossed the High Ridge and gone down into the veldt beyond had carried with them their primitive totemisms and spirit-worships, but many of their totemic animals were not native to the veldt and were forgotten, and the ancestors whom they had venerated on the benches of the High Ridge were buried there and their spirits could not follow into the plains. They came to worship the spirits of the warriors and wizards who had led them onto the veldt, and a pantheon of gods and goddesses no longer remembered as having been mortals gradually arose. Their worshippers were no longer Navvadrov; they had split into many tribes, and, with the domestication of pack and riding animals, wandered far.

A temple of the Mother-Goddess and a temple of Dindash stood side by side at Amarush; both were respected by the conqueror. The priests of Dindash traded generously for gold to enrich their altars. The first bits of copper and silver to reach Amarush went into vessels for both temples. For as long as Tammak I reigned, and Vallak I, his son, and through the reigns of Tammak II and Tammak III and Vallak II, there was peace in Amarush, though there was much fighting elsewhere on the river.

It was in the reign of Tammak IV that a trading town was established a hundred miles down-river from Amarush. Colonists came from Gvazol, an important town at the mouth of the river, and settled the town they called Gvazopinath. Their clear intention was to anticipate the upbound trade from the coast and break the monopoly of Amarush.

Tammak IV led an expedition against Gvazopinath before the thongs were dry on the roof-poles of the trading huts, and razed it to the ground. Unlike his illustrious ancestor, he spared neither the lives of the Navvazorf traders nor the temple of Dindash.

The next season, no traders came to Amarush. Instead, a fleet of fifty pirogues and rafts came up from Gvazol and attacked, attempting to put Amarush under siege. The siege lasted less than two weeks before the warriors from Gvazol were beaten off in a ruthless and bloody battle. Tammak IV immediately demolished the temple of Dindash in Amarush, taking its riches for the crown. The priests and the Gvazolla traders hiding in the temple he burned alive on a pyre beside the river, in a burlesque of the sacrifice ceremony to Dindash.

The Gvazolla attack had been voted on by the Gvazol village council and acted upon immediately. The warriors were an undisciplined mob without a semblance of leadership. For some time the thought had been abroad in Gvazol and the other coastal villages that they had outgrown their village-council government and communal economy. This crushing defeat, from which only fifteen of the fifty boats returned, converted thought into certainty.

"At Amarush," the survivors said, "Tammak is

king; all obey him. The Amarusholla fight as one, while we try to plan as one, but fight without a leader. Our fighting quickly becomes each-for-himself. We too must have a leader whom all will obey."

Two hot-seasons later a second expedition was led by a veteran river-trader and pirate-fighter named Shishdosh; he had twenty boats of Gvazol and five each from the neighboring villages of Trashol and Murshol. His warriors carried a new weapon: a sort of sword made by inserting rows of sharp flint into a thin hardwood board. They did not capture Amarush; the stockades built by Tammak I and strengthened by each of his successors were too strong. But while ten of the boats engaged the defenders in an arrow-fight at the front gate of the town, the others landed their boats out of bowshot and attacked on the leeward side, burning the fields of ripe grain, looting and firing the storage-sheds outside the walls, and making off with much spoil, including tools and weapons of a new, hard, brown metal that had come to Amarush from a village in the far uplands. They also captured twenty prisoners to bring back to Gvazol and sacrifice to Dindash.

The credit of Shishdosh stood extravagantly high after this exploit. When he began talking about another expedition, he was unanimously voted its chieftain. He began by gathering a personal staff of a dozen or so veterans of the previous expedition and appointing them sub-chieftains, responsible only to him. He further ingratiated himself with the priests of Dindash, imposed levies on the villagers, and put several dissenters to death in various showy manners; after which he effectively ruled Gvazol directly. The frightened, sycophantic village council was reduced to an advice-giving function, and Shishdosh seldom heeded its advice. On one pretext or another he managed to extend the period of preparation for the Great Raid for five flood-seasons.

Another village, Novzol, farther down the coast at the mouth of a smaller river, had begun trading with the Upland People several centuries before. A little below the head of pirogue navigation on their river they had found a Navvadrov village whose people had begun to mine and smelt copper. It was these people who learned to alloy it with other metals: silver, and tin, and zinc. By the time of Shishdosh's second expedition against Amarush, bronze tools and weapons were in limited use in the uplands and along the coast. Shishdosh himself carried a bronze sword with a double sawtooth edge, the appearance copied from the wood-and-flint weapons he had carried on his first campaign.

The Great Raid, five flood-seasons in the preparation, was successful. Shishdosh filled a number of captured Navvadrov canoes with his own warriors disguised in uplander skins and cloth caps. They raced ahead of his main fleet, simulating panic-stricken flight. Hastily beaching their canoes, this party rushed pell-mell for the gate, shouting that the Gvazolla war-party was behind them. Before the deception could be seen, the gate was opened for them and they swarmed in. The pirogues and rafts of Shishdosh's main fleet followed, landing their warriors directly in front of the gate. The disguised warriors kept the gate open until the main body could rush it and achieve a toehold inside the town itself. There was a desperate resistance, but in the end the defenders were wiped out or captured. Tammak IV himself was taken alive and then impaled on a great stake outside the front gate, where his body was left to swing in the wind for season after season until it finally disintegrated, and then the bones were gathered and mashed up, and the dust scattered.

Having tasted power, Shishdosh was loath to put aside the heady cup. Loading several pirogues with the richest loot, including bronze tools but no weapons, he sent them down the river in charge of a trusted henchman, inviting the priests of Dindash to come to Amarush and consecrate a new temple. While waiting, he strengthened the defences of the town, sent embassies to the adjoining upland chieftains, and recruited a company of Navvadrov archers. Then, after the consecration ceremony, he conferred the crown of Amarush upon Pinchidun, an old and trusted comrade, and returned to Gvazdol with his mercenaries and the Dindash priests. To keep order in Amarush, Pinchidun kept with him the warriors from the villages adjoining the Gvazol who had joined the expedition.

Back at Gvazol, Shishdosh entered the town triumphantly and immediately proclaimed himself king. The priests of Dindash annointed and crowned him, with the blessing of the Sun-God. Then, without even pausing to rest, he seized, one after the other, the three neighboring villages whose warriors were all still at Amarush keeping order, and added them to his kingdom.

Novzol, which had taken no part in the conquest of Amarush, was the main rival in prosperity of the new Gvazolla Kingdom. With bronze tools, the Novzolla had become skillful shipwrights. Their mariners learned to take advantage of the winds which rose after the hot season; instead of poling their small boats through the inland network of marshes and channels, they followed the coast, trading with other communities which were slowly changing from neolithic villages into mercantile cities. These, also, sent expeditions into the uplands in search of metals. Occasional wars broke out; alliances were formed and disintegrated. Finally, two centuries after the Shishdosh Dynasty came to power, Sharphad V of Novzol conquered Gvazol; shifting his capital to the city at the mouth of the Gvaru. Within a score of hot-seasons he had brought all the coastal cities into a single empire.

New methods were needed to handle increasing wealth and expanding trade. Gold—because it was universally valued, universally rare, and practically indestructible—became the standard of value. The art of writing and the science of mathematics were pressed into service in support of the empire, and were advanced and developed by the need for keeping increasingly complicated accounts and records. A new class grew up; humble scribes and bureaucrats, upon whose knowledge and administrative abilities the well-being of the empire depended.

Ships forced to sea by misadventure found the coasts of new continents: Dudak, to the north, and Zabash, to the south. Deliberate exploration followed accidental discovery; tribes of savages were encountered, with whom the explorers alternately fought and traded. The Coastal Empire grew, gradually and imperceptibly, into the first Sea Empire.

Chapter Five

The wandering gangs spread out across Hetaira, some to the Outer Hemisphere, but more toward the silver globe in the sky. They followed the game-herds in the plains beyond the Horizon Zone, first as foot-nomads, and then catching and breaking pack and riding animals, and driving game from one feeding ground to another. After generations in captivity, the descendants of these wild grazers and browsers had been selectively bred into domestic flocks and herds.

The larger and more prosperous gangs did not travel very far. They fought with one another over grass and water in the age-old manner of nomads, but tended to keep the peace when there was enough for all. They formed friendships and enmities and kept closely aware of one another by constantly meeting to trade and gossip. The smaller gangs, pushed out of the best grazing lands by their more numerous neighbors, invaded the mountain country around the Central Peak.

These displaced nomads found the country already peopled. Earlier gangs of paleolithic hunters had moved into the mountain valleys and up the rivers, and had discovered metals and something of how to use them. Little permanent communities, the first in the planet's history, had appeared at the richer ore-outcroppings; there would be houses around the mine-pits, and a furnace, and a forge. Hunting and food-gathering were still the chief occupation, but there would be some cultivation, and intermittent working of metal into tools and weapons.

Sometimes there would be bloody fights; more often the newcomers would trade cattle for metalware and carry it back to the plains, trading it for more cattle, and return then to the mountains to begin the cycle again. The miners and smiths came to depend less and less on hunting and farming, and more and more on being able to trade their work for foodstuffs.

There seems to have been no clearly defined demarcation between a Bronze and an Iron Age in Hetaira. As one community would learn to alloy copper, another would begin smelting and working iron. Even the carbonization of iron into steel came surprisingly early. The inquiring Hetairan mind, with its unceasing search for novelty, the ability to use existing knowledge to uncover new facts, all accelerated progress. Changes which might have taken millennia in another culture sometimes happened in decades on Hetaira. The wheel developed an axle shortly after it was first used as a roller under heavy objects. Almost at once it begot its numerous and varied progeny—the spinning-wheel, the potter's wheel, the water-wheel, the grindstone, the cart wheel. It gained spokes or teeth, and learned how to lift weights and turn cor-

ners; became the windmill, the bucket-chain, the
windlass, the pulley, and a variety of devices for
lifting or moving solids or liquids. Soon the
cartwheel gained an iron tire, and the plow an iron
plowshare; fields were cleared and roads were
built.

The communities were still based on gangs. Sexual promiscuity and the basic equality of the sexes
and lack of any sex-based division of labor prevented the development of anything like patriarchy
or matriarchy. There was little authority of any
sort, and no tyranny whatsoever. Once in a while
some individual would, by virtue of superior
strength or cunning, try to impose his will on others; such a one would invariably be found, in a
short time, laying in some field with an arrow in his
back. People deferred only to greater knowledge or
experience or inventiveness; and they had an uner-
ring ability to separate the gold from the dross.

What might be called capital property was usually owned in common by the gang; there were few
fixed rules of distribution, but there was very little
inequity or prolonged dissatisfaction with anything
within their control.

There would be long static periods, when
progress would slow down or stop its forward direction, allowing it to spread laterally among all
the people, and allowing complete exploration of
all the ramifications of some new discovery. Then
some new fact would be discovered in a totally new
direction, and there would be a frantic burst of invention to exploit it. The news of such discoveries
fairly flew from gang to gang. There were those
who made it their life's work to carry such news,

and they were welcome wherever they journeyed.

Talato Isleeta—Blazehead the Wanderer—had received his first name in childhood, from the wedge-shaped splash of pink fur that began at a point between his eyes and widened to cover the top of his head. He had made the second for himself; in his thirty years he had travelled completely around the Central Peak and up into the valleys of most of the rivers that flowed into the chaplet of lakes surrounding them. Usually, as now, he rode alone; his red-and-yellow lance pennon marking him as a wanderer, and therefore the carrier of no grudges, friendly to all who would have him visit, a non-participant in local feuds. He was usually welcome as a trader, story-teller, exchanger of information and news. Occasionally he would have to fight some outcast or small gang of marauders, as had happened only two sleep-periods ago; more occasionally some gang, for a private reason, would indicate that he was not, then, welcome in their midsts; but these happenings were rare, and he had enjoyed the hospitality of many gangs.

At the brow of the ridge, he reined in his *sorth;* the two plodding pack-animals behind him stopped also. There was a village in the valley below, as he had known there must be; the road had been freshly mended with logs and broken stone.

It seemed to be a mining and iron-working village; the mountains on both sides of the white-flecked, rocky river were gashed by the red scars of ore-workings. There was a bridge over the stream,

lifted above flood level on log piles, and at the far
end of it the village huddled around an open
square, houses on three sides, and on the fourth
two stubby furnace-stacks and a long forging-shop.
The stacks were smokeless now, and covered; the
anvils were silent, but there was considerable banging and clattering from the long shed that projected
to the river, the far end overhanging with a water-
wheel projecting from below. He could see figures
working on the slanting roofs of the houses. The
sun was approaching zenith—in a little while it
would be eclipsed by Shining Sister, which was
now lost in its glare, and then it would pass over
the top of Skystabber Mountain, and the hot time
would come, and the storms would follow.

Shaking his reins, he whistled softly between his
teeth. The *sorth* moved forward, and the two
toulths followed obediently, placid under their
loads of oilskin-wrapped packs. The bridge swayed
gently as they passed slowly over it. A villager met
him on the far side, as he passed between the
houses and reined up in the open square. He wore
a leather apron, a loincloth, and high buckskins,
and his fur was smudged with soot and scorched in
spots.

"I know you," the villager grinned. "I never saw
you before, but I know your name."

Talito passed his lance through the holding-strap
and slipped the butt into the socket on his stirrup
before dismounting. "Yes, I carry it with me," he
said, touching the pink blaze on his forehead.

"We have a couple of Talitos in our gang, too,
but there's only one Talito Isleeta. It is our pleasure to meet and speak with you. There was a girl

wanderer here a couple of hot-seasons ago who told us about you. She camped with you in a cave on Hornpeak through a storm."

Talito smiled. "Reeva Baleena," he said. "She plays a small harp and sings. She knows about medicines, and cures sick children. And she understands how animals must be bred for the qualities one wants."

"The same," the villager replied.

"A wonderful girl," Talito said. "I remember the three sleep-periods we were trapped by the storm with great fondness."

"We are the Tortromma Gang," the villager told him. "My name is Chwalvo. You want something to eat? We have a pot of stew on a fire in the forging shop. We're all staying there through the coming storm. It's the safest place, and we can make a fire without choking ourselves in the smoke. You can put your pack and things in there."

"Is there anything I can do to help you prepare?" Talito asked. "My *sorth* isn't any good for tethered work, but my *toulths* are broken to cart-harness."

Together they started for the long shed. "We have a lot of grain to cut and bring in," Chwalvo said. "It was late ripening this season. Our fields are as far up the road as you can drive a cart while you sing *The Song of the Four Foolish Hunters*."

Talito mentally ran through the song, with its twelve stanzas sandwiched between the three repeating verses. The field, he estimated, must be about ten hundreds of lance-lengths away. "You'll have your work cut out to get it all in before the storm," he said.

"Most of the children and old people are up there now," Chwalvo said, "cutting, threshing, and bagging. The pre-adults drive the grain carts."

Talito helped himself from the stew-pot on the fire and looked around the shadowy interior of the forge. A dozen or so able-bodied members of the gang had dismounted the water-wheel and were hoisting it above the anticipated flood level of the river. He saw something which interested him immediately—a framework of heavy beams supporting an iron hammer bigger than the body of a *sorth,* with a great log for a handle, pivoted more than halfway back, and set to be raised and released by a large, hooked cam operated by the water-wheel.

He gestured with his dagger, which had been halfway to his mouth with an impaled cube of meat. "That," he exclaimed. "That pounding contraption. I never saw anything like that before!"

Chwalvo grinned proudly. "I thought of it myself," he said proudly. "Ask any of the gang if I didn't. Are you going to make a picture of it? Reeva told us that's what you do when you find anything new; you make a picture of it with charcoal on skins and then tell people about it."

"I will probably do that," Talito said, going over to take a closer look at the apparatus. "It is very clever."

Chwalvo beamed. "Don't forget to say it was Chwalvo Tontrommo, at Red Gap Village, on Little Hoon River, who thought of making it. Are you going to make the picture now?"

"No, I'll have to see to my animals first. Then I'll take a cart out to the fields. Plenty of time for drawing after the work's done, when we're all in here together."

He helped the Tontrommo Gang get in their grain. When he was hungry, he ate from the big stewpot; when he was tired he spread his bedding on a pile of fresh straw and slept. The eclipse came while he was in the fields loading his cart with grain; the sun slid behind the disk of Shining Sister, the other world so like this one, so far away. The two worlds were flat plates, according to the best Hetairan theory, piled up with mountains in the middles. The sun went around them both, first one way and then the other. Shining Sister must be covered, at least on the bottom, with something bright, like silver. Talito wondered if there were people there too, and supposed that there probably were. They must be very different from his own kind; Shining Sister was so much closer to the sun that the heat there must be terrible.

The little river rose as the mountain glaciers began to melt. Everybody worked continuously until all the grain was harvested. The wind began blowing toward the advancing spot of heat as the sun slid over Skystabber; there was a period of calm while the sun was at zenith which lasted for a whole waking-period. Then the wind came howling down from the mountains. Broken branches and bits of debris rattled on the roof and hit the sides of the long forge-shop. Inside, it grew so dark that torches were lit. The children, frightened at the unaccustomed absence of light, whimpered and mewed, and the women and older youngsters comforted them. The rain came, first in wind-driven spattering, and then in a steady drumming, and finally in a continuous roar that drowned out even the thunder.

The rain continued for five sleep-periods. They sat around the fires, talking; they gathered to look at the things Talito produced from his trade-packs. Like all the *sorth*-riding wanderers, he carried only the lightest and most valuable wares, leaving the heavier and cheaper goods for the wagon-trains. There were several bolts of cloth he had gotten at a weavers' village across the ridge, but that was less than one waking-period's journey away, and the people of Tontrommo Village could get all of that sort of cloth they wanted.

They were fascinated, however, by the jars and cups and bowls of translucent, muddy-colored glass he had carefully packed in one of the oilskins. They had never seen glass before. They had never even heard of the village where the glassware had been made.

"Look, I'll show you." Talito took a roll of skin from a pack and opened it, spreading it before them. "Here, in the center, is Skystabber, with the other big mountains around it. The red arrow shows the direction the sun moves when the Bright Spot is in the sky with it; the black arrow shows the direction it moves when the Bright Spot appears as the sun sets. Here is where this village is." He took a small bottle and uncorked it, dipped a splinter into it, and made a few black marks on the map. "And here is Singing Trees Village, where I got that cloth. And Sand Hill Village, where they make vessels out of melted sand, is down here."

The Tontrommos stared at the map in happy surprise, exclaiming over it.

"Look, the squares are villages! And the wavy lines are streams, and the jagged lines are mountains. And these things, the circles with wavy lines in them—they must be lakes! Aren't they lakes, Talito? Why, this is wonderful! He has made a picture of the whole world, and whenever he finds a new place, he just marks it on; and he can see where everything is, and how to get from one place to another!"

"But what are all the strange squiggly marks that you have made all over the skin?" a girl asked, leaning over his shoulder.

"They're a kind of reminding mark," Talito explained to her. "See what I made for this village? A *tlinka*-leaf. *Tlinka* leaves are red. And this notched mark is my reminder for a gap. And here, by the water-mark, a *hoona* with a line over it, to show that it's little. Red Gap Village, on Little Hoona River. And a hammer under the village-square to show that this is an iron-working village."

"Look, Singing Trees Village!" The girl pointed. "There's a *ghinkeen*, because *ghinkeens* sing, and two trees next to each other, and the square village-sign. Singing Trees Village. And a loom under it!"

"Let me see!" one of the youths said, pushing forward. "Let me see if I can figure it out." He put his finger down on the map. "There's a village sign, with a *sorth* next to it—how clever; just three lines, and you can still tell it's a *sorth*—and wavy lines next to the *sorth*. Let's see; the wavy lines are water. The *sorth* is—what is a *sorth*? Green. Green Water Village?"

Talito smiled. "Nice try," he said. "And very close. You have the process right, you just guessed wrong about what a *sorth* means to me. Many things are green. What a *sorth* is, in my mind, is fast. That is Fast Waters Village, next to Fast Waters River. The river is very shallow, and the water in it moves very rapidly."

"Talito!" an elder toward the rear of the group cried out. "You must make us a world picture like this. If you do, we'll make something fine for you. What do you want in return? We could make you a dagger and a lance of a fine carbon-iron we have developed; many times stronger and a little lighter than the ones you now carry."

"The weight of my dagger is not excessive," Talito told him, "and my lance is of a strong, light wood and does not need to be of metal. But there is a weapon that I have wanted for some time, if it could be built."

"Well, if it *can* be built," the elder said, "we are the gang that can build it. What does it look like?"

"A long knife," Talito said, "with a blade as long as my leg from hip-joint to heel, double-edged, ridged in the middle to keep it stiff, and pointed. And a grip long enough so that I can swing it with both hands if I want to."

"For fighting on *sorth*back?" someone asked. "That sounds like a good idea. And you could use it with both hands on foot."

"But it would be too unwieldy," someone else objected. "It would be much too blade-heavy to move quickly."

"Why not lengthen the handle?" another Tontrommo suggested eagerly. "That would put weight at the rear to balance the blade."

"But the handle can't stick out too far in back,"

the first person said. "You'd have to hold your arms too far out to use the thing."

"A weight!" Chwalvo said, thumping his left hand into his right. "A ball of iron at the end of the handle to counterbalance the blade!"

"Copper instead of iron," the elder suggested. "It's heavier, so you'd need a smaller ball; and when it's polished, it's prettier."

Talito watched and listened curiously as this dialogue went on. It was rewarding to listen to such craftsmen as they went about solving problems. It was a pleasure to hear competent people display their competence. "I hadn't thought of that," he admitted. "The balance would be a serious problem. But now you've thought of it and solved it all in the space of time it takes a *sorth* to run ten lance-lengths. That is *exactly* what I'd like: a long iron knife counterweighted with a copper weight at the handle-end."

"We shall go to work on it right after the storm," the elder said. "We'll do a model in wood first, and weight it with lead to get the right balance. That way we can see how the shape should be for the best handling. *And* we'll find you a nice smooth white skin to make the world-picture on."

Talito dug into his pack and pulled out a big jar. "Here's something else I have," he said, taking the leather cover off. "Look at this."

He took out a pinch of white powder and mixed it carefully with about an equal amount of charcoal-dust. Then he scraped a flint along the roughened flat of his dagger to strike a spark. The mixture caught the spark about the third or fourth time he did it, and it sputtered, and then burned with a sputtery, smoky flame for four or five seconds.

"What do you think of that?" he asked.

"Will the flame catch dried grass?" a townsman asked.

"It will."

"Amazing! Tinder that blows itself on. Talito, where did you find such stuff?"

Talito pointed with his dagger to the map. "Down here on the Big Arrowwood River. It's found on the walls of caves. Do you want some?"

Chwalvo picked up a hammer from beside a small anvil. "Here, Talito, give us the weight of this, and we'll give you ten weights in worked steel: arrowheads, spear-heads, knife-blades, whatever you think you can use," he said. "This will be something to show people!"

"Well, don't eat any of it," Talito advised. "The Gobbilene Gang, who scrape this stuff off the cave walls and trade it, claim that if you eat it the girls will be disappointed in you for a while."

The girl beside Talito snuggled closer. "You haven't been eating any of it, have you, Wanderer?" she asked.

So the sword and the alphabet came to Hetaira, too. Talito's reminding-marks became ideographs; from them developed phonetic symbols. Talito's rolled skins were scraped down to parchments and vellums. Vegetable pulp was mashed up and spread on frames of finely-woven cloth for paper, and a variety of pens and inks were devised. And Talito's sword changed as it journeyed across Hetaira; the simple cross hilt became an elaborate basket-guard to protect the hand; and the blade assumed many different forms in different places, as the use of it and the method of handling it evolved. And then somebody added powdered sulfur to Talito's saltpeter and charcoal, and the sword became obsolete.

Chapter Six

The Bronze Age came more slowly to the Uplands of Thalassa, and to the veldt beyond the High Ridge. Forests gave way to fields; flocks and herds increased. Houses of adobe and kiln-hardened brick replaced log huts, behind walls of mud and stone. The nomads came in through the gaps of the High Ridge, driving herds of cattle and riding stock and pack animals to trade for tools and weapons of bronze, or slipped in small bands into the Navvadrov country to raid. They found deposits of copper and tin in the mountains of the second range, beyond the plains, and raiders brought back kidnapped Navvadrov miners and smiths, and in the process discovered and institutionalized slavery.

The Upland villages became towns and small cities, and the Upland tribes grew, slowly and without planning, into nations. As the nomad raids increased, permanent war-chiefs were appointed in each area, and patrols of warriors drawn from levies among the tribes. After a while the warriors were permanent also, supported by taxes paid to the war-chiefs. And so the war-chiefs became kings, and the warriors became a feudal nobility, each given a small area to live in and off of. These new kings quarreled bitterly with each other. Mud-walled towns were besieged, defended, taken, and retaken. The farmers sank into peasantry and, in some areas, to serfdom. The nomad raiders, growing more numerous, and thus stronger and more impudent, raided deeper and longer into the Upland while the kings and nobles fought among themselves.

Beyond the High Ridge, the nomad bands and tribes were combining, forming alliances and confederations. It remained for Krushpan the Shebb to unite them all under his leadership. He skillfully played tribe loyalty against tribe loyalty, and promises of loot from the Uplands, and position in his new federation of tribes, to get all the tribal sheiks to agree to come together under his supreme leadership. When he had assembled an army of twenty thousand, he led them through the passes of the High Ridge.

The moment was propitious. The army of Liapur had just taken, and was sacking, the town of Prehipur. Falling upon Liapur in the absence of its prince and its army, Krushpan's nomads looted it and enslaved its people. Then, rushing ahead of the news, his hard-riding warriors fell upon the victorious army of Liapur while it was still within the walls of Prehipur and still occupied with executing the last of Prehipur's defenders. Krushpan captured both the city of Prehipur and the army of Liapur without a struggle, his surprise was so complete, and annihilated both.

In the three years that followed, the nomads

made themselves masters of the Uplands on both sides of the Gvaru. Amarush, the now long-neglected outpost of the Sea Empire, fell with the rest.

The extinction of this foothold in the Uplands passed almost unnoticed by the people of the coast, whose eyes had long ago turned from the hinterland of Gvarda to the new lands across the sea. For the past century their colonies had been springing up everywhere—on Zabash, and Dudak, and Nimsh, and Vashtur. There was gold and silver on Zabash, and grain and wine-fruits. There was tin on Vashtur, and an animal with great teeth of ivory. There were oil-nuts on Nimsh, and copper, and in the mountains a reddish rock from which a new metal, gray and hard, was being smelted. And on Dudak were natives who made good slaves and were sold in herds in the markets of every city of the Empire.

The parent cities on Gvarda prospered. Their streets were paved with stone, and through them passed carts of merchandise, and gold-flashing chariots, and inlaid litters borne by slaves. The goods of every land piled the docks and crammed the warehouses. Merchants and nobles took their ease in the tapestried rooms of marble palaces, sipping the wines of Zabash and the fiery drink that the Dudak colony had learned to pot-still from the native beer. Music tinkled as harem beauties danced. Scholars in white robes sat surrounded by their disciples; statesmen met in council, and lords feasted. It was a good time; the sun of the Empire stood high.

The bright day ended with a thunderclap when

twelve ships of Novzol came foaming into Trashol
harbor, oars stroking to the double-beat of
hortators' drums, and brought the news that Novzol had fallen to an invasion of the barbarians of
the Uplands. Panic raced through the streets of
Trashol. Whips cracked as slaves toiled to raise
earthworks. Merchants and scribes and artisans
who had never shouldered a spear or cocked a
crossbow in their lives jostled into ill-formed ranks
under cursing decarians of the small professional
army. Altars smoked with sacrifices in the temples
of Dindash.

It was Gvazol itself, however, which fell next, before a boat-borne army from Amarush. There were
soldiers in Gvazol who could fight skillfully, and
citizens who fought bravely. The Emperor,
Ghrazhad IX, died at the head of his troops; the
High Priest of Dindash was cut down before his
altar. At the last, there was a frenzied stampede to
board the ships in the harbor. Some of them got
away, but many were capsized in the panic of the
crazed fugitives. Between one hot season and the
next, all the coastal cities of Gvarda were in
barbarian hands. The Uplanders looted and
burned them, hauled off their riches, drove the
people before them in slave-yokes, and returned to
the Uplands.

Ships, escaping from each coastal city as it fell,
brought a continuing rain of bad news to the or-
phaned colonies. Although the Empire, by any
practical standard, was still great, this blow produced a wound that would be centuries healing and
would never be forgotten. For the first time in
Thalassa's history, a fixed system of time-reckon-

ing was established by mutual consent, and a standard chronology emerged from the jumble of dates marking the reigns of kings. This was henceforth known as the Year One of the Downfall.

Vashtur had been colonized and was ruled by the hierarchy of Dindash; before the end of the Year One, the theocracy was split by sectarian schisms. On Dudak, the coast tribes who had been raiding the interior for captives to sell to the slavers, turned on their former customers. There were slave insurrections in the iron mines of Nimsh; escaped slaves, taking to the hills, taught the art of iron working to the local savages, and after a while these hill tribes, armed with weapons every bit as good as the colonists', became a serious threat to the peace. And everywhere spread, as though from some malevolent cloud, misfortune, poverty, and lethargic dispair.

After the conquest by Krushpan I, who had been born Krushpan the Shebb, and died Krushpan the Despoiler, the new masters of the Uplands had gradually forsaken their nomadic life, taking the towns and farmlands for their own. To the serfs and peasants, the conquest was merely an exchange of one tyrant for another. Krushpan's son, Tarask I, was a nomad shiek in a stone tent that could not be moved. His son, Krushpan II, was a king, with a brawling, disorderly nobility and a slave-holding aristocracy imposed on a still-alien population. There were intrigues and feuds. When Krushpan IV embarked upon the conquest of the coastal cities, it was less for the spoils than to divert his nobles from cutting each others throats and plotting to cut his. The new prosperity which came from this grandiose brigand-raid kept the Uplands quiet through the rest of his reign and through the reign of his son, Krushpan V. Then the fratricidal bickering began again.

Within a century the Upland Empire split along the line of the Gvaru River. Rapidly, even before war could break out between the two halves, both were convulsed by internal strife, and cracked into fractional kingdoms. Rowdy bands of nobles and their mercenaries burned, looted, and harried each others' lands and towns. The nomads from beyond the High Ridge—descendants of the stay-at-home cousins of Krushpan the Shebb—began raiding again. The mercenary companies, unpaid, deserted and pillaged the estates of their former employers until there was nothing left to take. Gradually peace—the peace of universal poverty and ignorance and apathy—came to the Uplands.

Slowly, the overseas colonies of the vanished Sea Empire dragged themselves up out of their dejection and began to re-build and look outward. The slave-trade from Dudak was revitalized, and ships began plying almong all the new states that had risen out of the debris of the Empire. With the renewal of commerce, piracy spread, and cities that had begun to trade with one another built war-fleets to protect their commerce.

In the year 783 of the Downfall, a ship from Tullon, on Nimsh, nosed into the silted harbor of Gvazol and found a berth beside an ancient wharf. She was one of a new class of men-of-war; probably the finest ships on the Central Sea. She had two banks of oars, and three masts with square-rigged sails, and could be sailed with reasonable confidence through the roughest weather. She had two decks, and a cargo hold below the oar-benches, and inclosed fore- and stern-castles. She had a sharp bronze ramming-prow, which was more for show than utility, and carried two big mangonels and a dozen deck-mounted catapults, constructed like giant crossbows.

Her captain went ashore, with his first officer and a scribe and a priest, followed by fifty sailors in steel caps and quilted jackets sewn with steel plates, who carried spears, crossbows, and short swords. They clanked through empty streets, between the ruined piles of great palaces; they came across broad squares filled with brush and tumbled statues; they stood among the vast ruins of the Temple of Dindash and looked up at the mutilated idol.

"What god did these people worship, Norgon?" the captain asked the priest.

"Probably the same one we do, under some other name, Zethron," the priest replied. "But whatever name it was is long forgotten. The gods have had so many names since the Empire fell. But under whatever name, the gods are still the gods."

So they made a fire on the tumbled altar and burned incense, and spilled wine, as one gives disguised alms to some impoverished nobleman, and went out.

Around Gvazol they found a wretched peasantry, huddled in mud huts or camped in ruined castles, scratching the ground with stone hoes. They had been citizens of the Empire once, and then slaves of the Uplanders, and now they owned themselves and their families, and some almost-useless stone tools, and nothing else. Going up river, the Tullonians found, at the mouth of a large tributary, a great mound of earth, with bits of rubble breaking through here and there, and more starving peasants. They did not know that they were looking at their world's first city, the capital in which had ruled their world's first king.

Returning to Tullon, Captain Zethron reported that he had found Gvarda worthless for conquest, colonization, or trade. The Council of Twelve accepted the report, but ignored the conclusion. There was much arable land, much grazing land, and a weak and docile population. Three years later, a fleet of twenty ships was fitted out, and the conquest of Gvarda was begun.

The Year 953 of the Downfall became the Year One of the Tullonian Empire. In that year, a fleet of six hundred ships, built in Tullonian and Tullonian-satellite yards, and carrying fifty thousand Tullonian and Gvardan soldiers, officered by Tullonian nobles, descended upon the coast of Zabash. Unlike the hordes of Krushpan I and Krushpan IV, they did not loot and burn and massacre indiscriminately. They seized the temples and treasure-houses; they put to death the Zabashan princes and installed puppets under Tullonian Viceroys; they levied taxes and imposed tributes, and conscripted soldiers.

The city-states of Vashtur and Dudak were frightened; ambassadors were exchanged and an alliance was formed. War flamed around the Central Sea; fleets of sailing-galleys smashed into one another, hurling missiles and fireballs. Vashtur and

Dudak made peace with the Empire, broke it, and went to war again. Vashtur was conquered; an army from Dudak invaded Gvarda.

By the fifth century of the Empire, the breakup had begun. In spite of the furious wars of the first and second centuries, the population had more than doubled. The Empire had engulfed three island-continents beside Nimsh, two of them rather large, and yet the sailing-galley and the wagon-train were still the best and most reliable means of transportation. The Empire, unable to police or protect or supply the area over which it had spread, simply began to come apart.

There was another Dudakan invasion of Gvarda; the provinces north of the Gvaru revolted and welcomed the invaders. At Tullon, an adventurer named Sarthon organized a conspiracy which resulted in the massacre of the Council of Twelve and his own seizure of power as dictator. Immediately Zabash rebelled and set up a Council of Twelve of its own as the true authority of the Empire. All Gvarda revolted a year later, and Gvarda and Dudak began a furious undeclared war against Zabash.

By the year of the Tullonian Empire 684, the second empire was as moribund as the first.

The Year 684 in the reckening of the Tullonian Empire would henceforth, over a large part of the inhabited globe, be counted as the Year One of The Books of Tissé.

Tissé was a shoemaker at Urava, on the continent of Dudak. He was frequently in trouble with the police, and his shop was a known gathering-place of the politically and socially disaffected. In addition, he was a violent dissenter from the locally established religion, and railed against the gods of Dudak and their priests, and against all polytheism and idolatry. There was but one god, Vran. Vran, and only Vran, had real existance, and all else existed only in the mind of Vran; in the memory of Vran the dead lived perpetually. One of Tissé's cronies was an unfrocked priest of Dudak. It is supposed that he contributed a great deal to this new religion. This ex-priest, Puzzá, did the actual writing of The Books, taking them down as Tissé dictated, sitting on one end of the cobbler's bench while Tissé worked at the other, with a pot of beer between them. Subsequent scholars claimed to be able to judge how nearly empty the pot was at the writing of any passage.

Although Puzzá later re-wrote The Books almost completely, they remained an ill-organized mass of moral preachments and mystical balderdash, written on so high an order of abstraction as to say all things to anyone who sought within their pages for Higher Enlightenment, and very little to anyone seeking logic, order, or common sense.

Heretofore, religious bigotry had been one evil from which Thalassa had been spared. Tisséism, with its doctrine of the one and only god, the *true* god, ended the old religious indifferentism and comparative tolerance. Any god but Vran was but a false idol; and therefore, any other worship was sinful, and imperiled the soul, not only of the idolator but of all those around him. Thus, persecution of the infidel became a religious duty.

* * *

In the beginning, the religion of Tissé marked a definite break with the old traditions; men's minds were wrenched from accustomed ruts and forced into new channels. There was, during the first four centuries of the Tisséan Era, a burst of invention and progress. Water and wind power were harnessed; a water-turbine was invented, and mountain streams were dammed to furnish the pressure to operate it. On Zabash, a crude steam turbine was invented.

Savagely persecuted at first, the followers of Tissé and his successor, Puzzá, involved themselves in politics out of self-defense. They entered into conspiracies to overthrow local governments. Where they failed, they were put to death in savagely spectacular fashion; where they succeeded, they were a powerful faction in the new government, if they did not control it outright. In some countries the worship of Vran was declared the only acceptable religion by the state.

These centuries were crowded with violence and tumult. Civil wars blazed; mobs howled in the streets and crossbow-bolts sleeted down on them; daggers were reddened in palace coups; partisan feuds smoldered and flamed. Kings were overthrown by dictators, dictators were toppled by popular revolt; democracies hardened into dictatorships or disintegrated into anarchy. And in every pot of violence that bubbled around the Central Sea, the religion of Tissé was always an ingredient.

Four centuries later, the social system solidified again. With the exception of heretical splinter sects, the Creed of Puzzá was the universal form of Tisséism. Its priests turned ever sterner faces upon innovation; they themselves had become the conservators of tradition. The bourgeoisie who had come into secular power during the previous four hundred years had become no less reactionary. Powerful guilds had sprung up in all the mercantile cities around the Central Sea; having gained wealth by the skills and inventiveness of their fathers, they were loath to encourage any sort of innovation which might threaten their own status. Technical improvements were suppressed or shrouded in guild secrecy. The great slave-holding nobles saw the new machinery as replacing the slave-labor in which their wealth was invested. For another seven centuries the city-states and kingdoms, which were the remnants of the old Tullonian Empire, lived in the gloom of stultifying rigidity in social conditions, actions, and thought. New ideas were ruthlessly suppressed, and the only change was in the names of the overlords.

Then, in the year 1275 of The Books of Tissé, another book was published on Dudak—and it was called *The Confessions of Zaithu.*

Chapter Seven

The little villages of the craftsmen-gangs around Hetaira's Central Peaks were visited regularly by the wagons and pack trains of traders, and by the occasional lone wanderer. The traders adopted the custom of establishing permanent base-camps at which they could store goods, and these in time grew into market towns. The wanderers had their rendezvous places too, where they met and exchanged news, and left messages for one another. At first such places were caves or other natural shelters, or merely stone cairns in which messages could be left. Occasionally a wanderer, crippled or immobilized by age, would make his home by one of these rendezvous-points in order to keep in touch with his life-long friends, and perhaps perform a useful service for them. The wanderers, glad of a warm place to stay, and a secure depository for their messages, and perhaps even some of their goods, happily supported these way-stations.

It became customary in many gangs for a few of their youngsters to wander for a time, meeting new people and learning new things. It was soon discovered that more could be learned by the young people going to the nearest of the wanderers' rendezvous, to stay with the resident and meet the life-long wanderers passing through. The youths would pay for their keep by hunting, and farming, and doing housekeeping chores. Soon every young Hetairan of the Central Mountain country was spending at least the time between two hot-seasons at some rendezvous. The rendezvous grew, some of them arranging with wanderers to visit at periodic intervals especially to teach. These places became libraries, museums, institutes of technology, and eventually universities. It was at one of them that a steam-engine for propelling barges on the lakes was invented; at another, firearms were developed.

Civilization spread more slowly on the plains between the mountains and the Horizon Zone. The nomadic herders became settled ranchers, trading livestock and hides for manufactured goods through the wagon-traders. Unsuccessful ranching gangs became bandits and cattle-rustlers; the plains country was full of violent crime, and violent justice.

The Horizon Zone developed a culture similar in pattern to that of the Central Mountains, although always a few score years behind. Communities were isolated, dispersed in a narrow ribbon forty thousand kilometers around the planet. There were wanderers and wanderers' rendezvous there, too; but news travelled more slowly and less certainly.

In the Outer Hemisphere there were more nomads; the mountains and uplands were thinly peopled by gangs of hunters and farmers, and a few gangs roved around the shores of the Central Sea.

When the Central Mountain people of the Inner Hemisphere were working steel, the Horizon Zone had barely progressed to the use of metals, and the whole Outer Hemisphere was still paleolithic. When the Central Mountain country had the musket in common use, and was investigating the advantages of rifling the barrels, the bow was still widely used in the Horizon Zone. As for the people of the Outer Hemisphere, it was not until the railroads were extended into their country that they emerged from the Bronze and Early Iron Age.

The first railroad was the Red Lake To Sulfur River; it was seven hundred and twenty kilometers in length, single-track. Its rolling stock consisted of two wood-burning locomotives and about forty cars. There was a daily train in each direction; cannon were fired as they passed signal-points, to warn the oncoming train to back to the nearest switch-out.

There had been no system of historical reckoning on Hetaira until then, and no need for any; but the gang that built the Red Lake To Sulfur River realized that now some method of accounting for the passage of time, both sleeping-period to sleeping-period and season to season, would be needed. And so, with proper pomp and ceremony, when the first train left the steamboat landing at Nardavo's Town for the headwaters of the river, they proclaimed the Year One of the Railroad. [As nearly as can be determined, this corresponded with the year 2264 of the vanished Tullonian Empire, or the year 1522 of The Books of Tissé.]

Standing at the foot of the gangplank with the

other passengers who had disembarked at Nardavo's Town, Dwallo Dammando looked around the wharf curiously, examining the piles of cargo waiting to be loaded for the return trip across Red Lake. Bagged grain, and kegs of spirits; bales of furs from the mountains; barrels of refined sulfur; bales of cloth; bar iron and steel; crates of straw-packed glassware. No wonder the wagon-train gangs were cursing the Bollardo Gang and their railroad.

The luggage-wagon, drawn by a pair of *toulths*, came down the ramp; along with the fifty odd other passengers, he fell in behind it. The driver was one of the Brancanno Gang, who ran the steamboat, but he couldn't be expected to know the ownership or look after the safety of every box and bag and bed-roll on the wagon. It was a good idea to keep a close watch on your own belongings.

"I'm going to the market first," the driver told them. "Wagons there for Sweetwater, across the isthmus, and up Crooked River. If you're taking the railroad, leave your things on the wagon; I'll take them to the platform next. Train leaves in about an hour."

The market was an open square, surrounded by buildings of stone and brick and plank. A few were old, most of them were new, and several were still being built. There were warehouses, and a tavern, and trading markets with open fronts and plank marquees which could be lowered on chains during the rains. Fifteen or twenty big transport wagons, with double-rows of passenger-seats atop their cargo bays, stood in the middle; some seemed to have arrived only recently, for their freight was piled beside them, and the traders were dickering over it. One wagon had attracted a number of dickerers; its load consisted of square wooden boxes, all painted with the glyph of the Sambro Gang, and lettered, in phonetic alphabet, Rifle Number 2, Rifle Number 3, Revolving-chambered Handgun Number 3.

"No, we won't take grain," one of the wagon gang was saying, as Dwallo came within hearing. "By the time we got to Sweetwater, the *toulths* would have the whole load eaten. Besides, one case of cartridges is worth a whole bin-load of grain."

"Well, will you take an order on the Yavanno Gang for twenty loads of grain for twenty cases of cartridges?" one of the local merchants asked. "You can trade that for anything you want, either here at Nardavo's, or at Sweetwater."

"Three barrels of brandy for two cases of Rifle Number Three!" another merchant shouted.

The baggage-wagon rolled past and stopped. Men and women from different transport gangs detached themselves from their wagons and ran over, shouting:

"Raldarro Gang for Sweetwater!"

"Luilloro Gang, up Crooked River; what'll you trade for a ride?"

"For Sweetwater, Kalvanno Gang. Padded seats and good springs on the wagon! Leaving in an hour!"

The steamboat passengers who were taking wagons began to pull their bags and bedrolls out of the pile on the wagon. Dwallo, watching the rectangular leather-covered case and the bed-roll with his name painted on them, did not notice the shabby little fellow in the *sorth*-skin trunks and tattered canvas vest dart away. Suddenly, from the other side of the wagon, a voice shouted:

"Drop that bag, you thieving *rogel,* or I'll drop you with it!"

As the fellow broke into a run, Dwallo noticed him, and saw that his third piece of luggage, the shoulder-bag that contained his trading items, was in the thief's hand. He grabbed for the heavy revolver at his hip, but before he could draw it, a rifle cracked, and the thief leaped into the air and fell dead. As he went around the tail of the wagon, another man appeared from the far side, a heavy rifle smoking in his hands. They both reached the body at the same time.

"A good shot, my friend," Dwallo said. "My thanks." He stooped and retrieved the bag. "I should have kept hold of this in the first place."

The stranger, a man in white *hoona*-leather trousers and vest, worked the lever on his rifle, picked up the empty cartridge and pocketed it, and smiled. "For nothing, your thanks. You would have shot anyone you saw stealing my belongings. Anybody would. See a thief and fail to shoot him, and you only encourage the breed."

"Nevertheless, my thanks for it," Dwallo said. "And my hand. Dwallo Dammando," he introduced himself.

"Koshtro Evarro," the other said. "You're going on the railroad? So am I."

They fell into step, following the wagon to the railroad platform. An old man who walked with a limp, and a slender, rather tall girl came over while the luggage was being unloaded. Both wore canvas coveralls to keep their fur clean, and carried revolvers on their hips.

"It's all right to leave your stuff here," the limp-

ing man said. "The Bollardo Gang's responsible
for it until you leave the train."

The girl took their destinations and chalked
them on the luggage, then she led the passengers
over to a table and sat down.

"Four prime *toulth*-hides for the trip to
Nandrovvo's for the two of us?" a man asked.

When the girl agreed, he showed her a warehouse receipt, and wrote out an order on a local
brokerage and storage gang. Another passenger
produced a jug of brandy; the girl uncorked it,
smelled it, and accepted it for passage. Dwallo
pulled a book out of his shoulder-bag and handed
it to her.

"How about this, for a trip to Vallado's Village?" he asked.

"Oh, that's too much," she protested, "we're not
robbers!" Then she looked at the title-page. "I
thought I recognized your name when I saw it on
your things. You can ride with us for nothing;
we're all proud of the book your gang printed
about our railroad."

"No, take the book," Dwallo insisted. "I don't
think you have it; we just printed it."

She looked at it again. "*The New Steam Engine
Which Re-condenses Water More Efficiently, Designed by Johas Mandorgo at Needle Rock Rendezvous, as Described by the Designer,*" she read.
"No, I've never heard of it. Thank you, Dwallo."

"And here; here's a list of the new books our
gang has printed this past season," Dwallo added.
"Take it and show it to your gang. Maybe you'll
want to order some of them."

"I'm sure we would. How long are you staying at

Vallado? We'll have a list of what we want ready for you when you pass through here again."

With his new-found friend Koshtro, Dwallo examined the train which was waiting at the platform. Although he had made the cuts of the drawings to illustrate the book his gang had published, Dwallo had never seen the actual locomotive and cars before. The locomotive was like a miniature steamboat engine, with a brick furnace and a sheet-iron boiler, mounted on a wheeled platform of iron-plated timbers, with the stack and the two cylinders in front. Behind it was the fuel wagon, which could hold either wood or coal, and the freight wagons, and the two passenger wagons at the rear. The wheels had wide flanged iron tires; the track was built of squared timbers, faced with angle-iron on the inside. While Dwallo was examining the train, the little cannon on the platform boomed. He and Koshto hastened to get seats in one of the passenger wagons.

"I'm from the Sky Lake country," Koshto told him. "I have the book your gang printed about the railroad. My gang and a couple of other farming gangs are teaming together to build a railroad of our own. We have a wonderful country for grain, but we've no place to trade it close enough for the wagon-trains. We make a little whiskey, but we can only trade so much of that; they raise sugar-roots on one side of us, and make rum, and they make fruit-brandy on the other side of us. So we decided to build a railroad, and I was sent up here to study this one.

"I've been here at Nardavo's three days," he continued. "I don't like this town. That fellow who tried to steal your bag was the fifth thief I've seen shot in these three days. The first one I've shot myself, but still—

"I've also seen maybe a dozen brawls, three or four of them serious enough to kill a person or two. There are too many gangs in this town, and none of them willing to see to it that things are kept peaceful. I'm going to recommend that the gangs in our railroad, when we get it built, see to keeping order in our railhead town. Any other gangs who want to come in can do so like trading-gangs in a craftsmen's village, on the understanding that they're guests, and have to behave themselves."

The locomotive made a series of whooshing sounds, and then the train gave a couple of jerks, a jolt or two, and started creeping forward. "I noticed that there was a big crowd in town, seemed to be just standing around fingering their rifles and waiting for something to happen," Dwallo said as the train picked up speed.

"Oh, that. That's on account of the Thurkkas," Koshtro told him. "You've heard about that?" Dwallo shook his head. "Savages from over on the other side of the Rim Country," Koshtro went on to enlighten him. "There's been bad times over there—drought, cattle-plagues, gang-wars—and thousands of those people have migrated. They went through the Rim Country and onto the plains on this side. The ranching gangs wouldn't let them settle there; pushed them on, and they've come on into the Central Mountain country. About a thousand of them came down Crooked River; the gangs upstream didn't try to stop them, so they're camped below the lowest village on Crooked

River, and starting to move into the isthmus. The gangs up Sulfur River are determined not to let them through; all the gangs have sent people to ride patrol and stop them."

Koshtro was riding to the end of the line, to get a look at the Bollardo Gang's repair shops. Dwallo bid him goodbye at Vallado's Village and got off. The Vallado Gang lived in a number of big barn-like houses against the side of the mountain; their furnaces and forge and rolling-mill were a kilo-meter up the river; there was a trestle-bridge carry-ing a track to and from the ore-pits. The furnace-stacks were blazing, and a couple of heavy drop-hammers boomed intermittently. A half-grown youngster helped him up the path to the houses with his box and bedroll.

A girl met him on the wide veranda as he climbed the front steps. He introduced himself and asked if Kursallo Vallado were about.

"He's up at the works," she said. "He'll be com-ing down in a few hours. I'm Sharra; Kursallo's mother and mine are sisters. He's told us about you, from the time you were at Mirror Lake Ren-dezvous with him. And we have a lot of books your gang printed."

She and the youngster helped him in with his things. She showed him the room where he could sleep, and the bath, where fifteen or twenty of the gang, who had just come from the furnaces, were washing the soot out of each other's fur with a fresh-smelling soap. He ate with this group, and later Sharra and several others showed him around the living quarters and the works, and the mines across the river.

"My gang needs a new printing-machine," Dwallo told his friend Kursallo, as they and a dozen others sat on the west veranda, out of the glare of the sun. "We decided to contract your gang to make it because we like your work on heavy machinery, and because we could get it quicker and safer from you over the railroad. This will be a big machine; it's to be run by steam instead of by hand."

"I never heard of a printing-machine run by steam," one of the older Vallados said. "Something that's just been invented?"

"Yes, we invented it ourselves. You see, the paper-making gang we trade with has invented a way of making paper in long rolls instead of sheets. They can make, in one strip, enough paper to reach from here to the railroad station," Dwallo said.

There were exclamations of surprise, but not of incredulity. If Dwallo had said that somebody could make a strip of paper long enough to reach to Shining Sister, it would have been accepted. People simply did not make statements that were contrary to fact.

One of the younger men nodded thoughtfully. "So, if you have a long strip of paper, on a roll, you'd run it between two rollers with the type on them. How wide is this roll of paper?"

"About two arms-widths," Dwallo said, holding his arms wide apart.

The young man nodded again. "Yes," he said. "For that you'd need steam-power. It would take the strength of fifty *toulths*, at least. What sort of steam-engine are you going to use? We have a nice design that might be appropriate. Do you want us to build one for you?"

"No. We have a used engine from a steamboat that wrecked itself below Klamdammo's Landing. The Kwissato Gang salvaged it for us. Very clever job, too. We're doing a book about their methods. But we will need the printing machine built entirely." He picked up a leather tube he had brought out onto the veranda with him; pulling off the cap, he withdrew a roll of thin paper. "Here are the plans for it."

They were passed from hand to hand, among much murmuring and continuous appreciative exclamations.

"This is good designing, Dwallo," Kursallo approved. "With a machine like this, you could print more books in one waking-period than you could make by hand in a sun-trip!"

"We anticipate a problem in keeping up with the job of binding all the books we expect to print with this new machine," Dwallo said. "But that's the sort of problem we like."

"There's only one thing, Dwallo," one of the older women said. "I don't know whether we can make this printing machine or not. Not that we lack the skill—I'll take a bath in the blood of whoever claims that! But we lack the time and the hands. It's getting harder every year to work the ore pits, and if we put enough of our people to mining, we don't have enough to work the furnaces. And about a third of our gang are carrying rifles on the isthmus, riding patrol against the Thurkkas."

"And then the Bollardos are going to build another line, from Red Lake to Sweetwater," another said. "They're going to need facing for seventy-five thousand lances of track, and two new engines, and a lot of wagons. They want to do that in three years, too—"

Dwallo took back his plans and spread them out in front of him. "I'm sorry to hear all of this," he said. "We've really planned on having this new printing-machine, and I would be happier with your gang doing it. Now let me see; we can use timber for some of this, and we have a few of our own good blacksmiths who can forge most of the smaller parts. I'll go over these plans again and cut the work for you down to what we just cannot do ourselves . . . Incidentally, I have some new books in that leather box. Why don't you look through it while I make some preliminary notes."

As soon as the box was opened, Kursallo snatched a copy of the steam-engine book, leafing through it very rapidly. "I want one of these, Dwallo!" he exclaimed.

"Oh, here's something I want!" Sharra cried, taking another book. "I never imagined there was such a book!"

Dwallo glanced up to look at the cover: *A History of the Different Attempts to Scale the Peak of Skystabber,* he read. "Yes, that was printed only three sun-trips ago. Are you interested in mountain climbing?"

"In climbing Skystabber, yes. The highest place in the world, right under Shining Sister." She looked up at the pale silver globe in the sky, and then to the distant horizon. "You can see Skystabber from here—there, in the notch at the head of the valley. Some day I'm going to climb it."

During the next two waking periods, Dwallo made other trips around the Vallado Gang's ore-pits, smelters, and steel-works. The ore-pits, worked continuously for centuries, had gone deep into the mountains; they were becoming progressively harder to mine. The Vallados were working hard, by any standard acceptable to any craftsmen's gang—at least a quarter of the time—sleep periods included. And of the two-hundred-odd members of the gang, at least seventy were out riding patrol on the isthmus against the Thurkka menace.

The second train in from Red Lake after Dwallo's arrival brought news of fighting. The Thurkkas had made a mass drive toward a thinly-guarded stretch of open country on the left of Crooked River. Only the arrival of a large party from Nardavo's Town, with the cannon from the railroad station, had stopped them; and at that one band of several hundred had broken through and were camped on a rocky hill inside the isthmus.

There was a mass-meeting of the Vallados to decide whether they should send reinforcements, and whom they could spare. As he listened to the arguments, an idea suddenly struck Dwallo.

"Will you let an outsider offer a word?" he asked. "Then, instead of trying to wipe these Thurkkas out, why don't you bring a couple of hundred of them here, and put them to work in your ore-pits? Feed them, and let them earn their food by digging ore for you. They were probably hard workers until the drought forced them out of their homes."

"You mean take these savages into our gang?"

somebody shouted in horror.

"Certainly not! Let them form a gang of their own to work for you. Trade them for their work under a definite contract. Furnish them tools, and give them so much in trade for every cartload of ore they dig. And you could let them do shovel-work around the furnaces, too. That way your own gang would be free to do the real work at the mill and the forges."

There was silence for a moment. "Maybe it would work, at that," one of the older men considered. "Digging ore and shoveling coal is nothing but *toulth* work. Why, if we had a couple of hundred of those people in the ore-pits and on the coal-pile, we could build another furnace and put in a couple more hammers."

"We'd need a few of our people to show them what to do, and fire the blasting-shots, of course—"

Dwallo said nothing else. His suggestion had caught the imagination of the Vallados. Now they'd be able to build his power-driven printing-machine, and his gang would be trading books all around the Central Mountains.

It never occurred to him that he had just invented the wage system.

Chapter Eight

Zaithu was an apostate Puzzán priest, as Puzzá himself had been a renegade from the earlier polytheism. It was his thesis that Puzzá had been an impudent and sacrilegious pretender and that his self-styled Successors were blasphemers and perverters of the Sacred Truth. That truth, Zaithu held, was found only in The Books of Tissé, and the individual, equal in the Mind of Vran with all others, must interpret them according to his own conscience. Instead of solemn liturgies, the religious services of Zaithu's followers consisted simply of readings from and discussions of The Books; whenever disagreement grew too passionate over some obscure passage, the service-leader—elected by the congregation; there were no separate priests —would call for prayer and meditation.

The new religion took liberty-loving Dudak by storm, in spite of all that the Puzzán hierarchy could do. A series of bitter religious wars blazed up; in the end the Successor, Glavrad XXII, and his council of Archpriests, were expelled and sought refuge at Tullon, the now-decayed seat of the ancient Empire. Freed from the strangling toils of religious absolutism, and lacking any powerful feudal nobility or any strong guild tradition, Dudak plunged into a cultural and technological renaissance.

The two smaller continents of Gir-Zashon and Thurv, screened by Nimsh and Vashtur from the Central Sea, had been discovered in the third century of the Tissén Era; the discoverers had been pirates, interested only in a safe base of depredations. They had made friends, and finally amalgamated with, the natives, a barbarian race calling themselves the Hoz-Hozgaz, and had taught them the arts of civilization. In time, the descendants of the Hoz-Hozgaz and their pirate mentors turned from the sea and began exploiting the interior of Gir-Zashon and exploring the neighboring continent of Thurv, forgotten by the busy world around the Central Sea.

If they were forgotten, they were nonetheless not allowed to forget that world. Refugees trickled across the straits, seeking a haven from war and persecution, bringing news. One of these refugees described the steam-turbine engine which had been built on Zabash. He had been foreman in a construction crew which built a few of them. Within his lifetime, he saw hundreds of them in operation on Gir-Zashon, and died rich and honored as a result. One of the Hoz-Hozgaz who had become interested in this new source of power began using briquettes of charcoal mixed with fish-oil for fuel; another discovered a method of refining fish-oil and invented a burner for it.

On Dudak, too, the steam-turbine found favor. There the fuel problem—the turbine is a hungry beast—was solved in the dense jungles along the inner coast, where two growing-seasons a year provided unlimited fermentable vegetable matter. The Dudakans invented an alcohol-burner and became distillers instead of fishermen. They also invented a steam-jet engine for ship propulsion.

The old rigid world of feudal estates and mercantile guilds shattered like glass all around the Central Sea. Merchants fumed, lords and kings stormed, priests thundered anathemas—but the ships of Dudak could outsail the merchantmen and outfight the war-galleys of Zabash and Vashtur and Nimsh. They could only be met by imitation and improvement. And so, in every kingdom and city-state, for self-preservation, steam-turbines and steam-jet engines and ships of the new pattern were being built.

The search for sources of fuel became frantic. Dudak and Gvarda, now co-religionists and allies, controlled the alcohol-producing jungles. Zabash took to the sea with a fleet of trawlers, and, unable to get sufficient fish-oil from the Central Sea, pushed out into the unknown waters beyond the ring of continents. Some ships, venturing far beyond the accepted limits of safety, found a chain of reefs and islands encircling the Horizon Zone. It was these venturesome seamen, first of all Thalassans, who sighted the globe of Hetaira on the distant skyline.

On Vashtur, in search of new fuels, the properties of potassium nitrate were discovered, as Talito Isleeta had demonstrated them almost two thousand years before and a quarter of a million kilometers away on Hetaira. On Vashtur, too, somebody tried a mixture of charcoal, sulfur, and saltpeter. Unfortunately, a fairly large batch was mixed in a fairly deep vessel. One of the survivors, fleeing an accusation of sorcery, carried an account of the experiment to Gir-Zashon. The Hoz-Hozgaz were deeply interested; they had access to large deposits of both sulfur and nitrates. In a short time they developed a really reliable black powder mixture. It was first used in bombs, to be thrown from mangonels; somebody found out how to make rockets, and shortly after somebody else deduced the principle of the gun.

By this time the ships of Zabash were making regular trips to the Outward Islands. On several of the larger, where there was fresh water and vegetation, they established fishing bases and oil refineries. Their ships began venturing beyond the islands and into the Ocean Sea, where they discovered sea-monsters of a size hitherto undreamed of; things bigger than the largest ship, against which skippers sometimes were forced to use their mangonels and catapults, when the beasts got too inquisitive. Many ships never came back from such encounters, but a few returned towing gigantic corpses from which enough oil would be tried and refined to load the largest tanker.

The people of Gir-Zashon and Thurv, too, built steam-jet ships; they established bases and refineries in the Outward Islands. Word had reached them of the monsters of the Ocean Sea, and they fitted out ships to hunt them and kill them with rockets and gunfire. It was some time before the Zabashans learned of the new weapons developed on Gir-Zashon, but in time they were compounding gunpowder and arming their ships with cannon.

Collisions between fishing fleets occurred. For the first time in Thalassan history, guns thundered back and forth in sea-battles, and rockets left their fiery trails. Armored warships appeared, hunting fishermen instead of fish. A flotilla of gunboats from Zabash caught and destroyed a fishing fleet of Gir-Zashon; a Hoz-Hozgaz fleet, striking at a Zabashan base while the fishing-boats and gunboats were away, massacred the inhabitants, filled their tanks with oil, and blew up or burned the installations. When the news of this action got back to Karkasha, the capital of Gir-Zashon, another fleet was sent to forestall retalliation by attacking the Zabashan naval base of Harsh. The Fish Oil War had finally reached the Central Sea.

Chapter Nine

With the labor of two hundred hired Thurkkas, the Vallado Gang was so able to increase production that the Bollardo Gang finished the Sweetwater branch of the Red Lake To Sulfur River Railroad by the year 14, using another eight hundred Thurkkas as track-laborers. These, on completion of the work, migrated to Sky Lake in time to help complete the railroad Koshtro Evarro and his associates were building. The Sky Lake Line was finished in the Year 16.

In the Year 22, a combination of wagon-trading gangs, discerning the shape of the future, built a railroad to connect the Sky Lake Line with the Bollardos' Sweetwater Branch. Halfway around the Central Mountains, three more railroads began building, sending to the Rim Country for more laborers. A line was built in the Rim Country in 54, extending almost fifteen hundred kilometers; in 78, the Central Mountains had been almost completely girdled, and the old tracks of iron-faced timbers were being rapidly replaced by steel rails. In 84, the Short Circle Line was built by a combination of railroad gangs; three thousand kilometers in length, it went completely around the great peaks at the middle of the mountain country, connecting with all the lines running in from the lake country.

As railroads and lake steamboats multiplied, outlets were provided for more and more goods. The Vallado Gang, for example, were forced to invent and build steam-shovels to facilitate mining, and to construct a railroad of their own to the source of Sulfur River to open new ore-pits. By this time, they had come to concentrate almost entirely upon rails, engines, and heavy machinery.

Small manufacturing gangs, depending upon local trade, began to vanish. Some merged with other gangs; some, unable to keep abreast of the changing industrial pattern, went out of business, their members going to work for wages for other gangs. A few concentrated upon quality handcrafts for a growing luxury trade; the artist as distinct from the artisan began to come into his own.

Wage-employment became more and more common, although the working out of barter-wages sometimes became incredibly complex in this society without money. The cleavage between labor and ownership grew sharper with the growing importance of the industrial plant, and the member of a hired gang watched, with each year, the increase of wealth which he had produced but in which he did not share. Resentment smouldered; for the first time Hetaira was experiencing what might be called a genuine class-struggle. There was even job-competition; gangs of migratory workers in the agricultural and construction trades fought over employment, sometimes so bitterly that the survivors of two contending gangs would be barely enough

for the available jobs. By the end of the Second
Century of the Railroad, almost every industry was
employing hired workers.

Among these, the idea began to spread that anybody who did work, at least on a permanent basis,
for a gang, should be allowed to join that gang.
There were demands for larger and larger shares in
the profits, and refusals to work when these demands were not met. There was fighting when
gangs of migratory workers were hired to replace
the strikers. There were campaigns of sabotage,
pilferage and shirking. There were strikes in which
the workers occupied their places of employment
and refused admittance to their employers; and
when the employing gangs tried to prevent workers
from bringing food and arms with them to work,
there was more trouble. Occasionally a band of dis-
satisfied workers would form around the nucleus
of a small manufacturing gang being forced out of
business and organize a gang in competition with
their former employers; then there would be shoot-
ings and raids and bombings and arson.

The apex of violence was reached in 206, in the
Sugar Valley Massacre. A fairly small but wealthy
gang of sugar-root planters, the Halzorro Gang,
employed over a thousand workers, having cleared
an entire valley and planted it in sugar-root. They
had refineries and a distillery, and a railroad of
their own to get their sugar and rum to market.
While there had never been a page of Hetairan history defaced by any record of actual chattel
slavery, conditions on the Halzorro plantations
came nastily close to it. The Halzorros had even
hired a gang of bandits to help them bully their

workers into submission. They overreached themselves, however, when they tried to disarm the workers. Nothing of the sort had ever been heard of before; on Hetaira, the right to keep and bear arms was equivalent to the right to breathe.

Rebellion exploded instantly; inside half a waking-period the workers had killed all the Halzorros, to the youngest child, and all their hired bravos, and had taken the plantation. There was no destruction or looting or needless brutality; when the last Halzorro was dead, the workers returned quietly to their tasks, this time as owners. No authority existed to which anybody could appeal, were there anybody left to appeal; each gang was sovereign, and the sovereign Halzorros had been overthrown by revolution. The victors adopted the style of the Halzorro Gang and continued doing business under it.

Less violently, the same process had been going on everywhere. The Vallado Gang, a quarter of a century before, had admitted all their workers to gang membership. Neither the railroad gangs nor the Telegraph Gang had ever used wage-workers except on temporary construction jobs, and construction gangs had long ago become contractors, with their own tools, carts, *toulths,* and even steam-shovels, steam-rollers, and steam-tractors. The wage system, having served its purpose in the industrialization of Hetaira, decayed and vanished even before the invention of money.

Sharra Vallado joined in an attempt to scale Skystabber in the Year of the Railroad 17. It was a well-equipped expedition, all veteran climbers, but it was brought to a stop on the north wall, at the second bench from the top. Four years later she made another attempt; of a party of eight, only she and two others returned alive. She made her final attempt in 27, accompanied only by two novice climbers. None of the three was seen again alive. The bodies of her companions were found two years later after a snow-slide; in 122, the Paldonno Expedition found Sharra Vallado's remains on a ledge, within a thousand feet of the summit, identifying her by her rusted ice-axe and a silver belt-buckle. They, themselves, could climb no higher. They cut her name and gang-symbol into the rock, left her bones where she had stopped using them, and carried down her axe, buckle, and rusted dirk, and deposited them in the museum at the Climbers' Rendezvous.

It was the Kalgravno Expedition, in 277, which finally reached the summit. Eight students and two instructors from the Kalgravno Rendezvous, in Traplino Valley, made their climb along the south face and crawled up a slanting knife-edged ridge until they found a crack extending all the way to the top of the highest spire. From below, the spire had seemed as sharp as a needle, but when they reached it they found, at the very tip, a cuplike depression almost fifty lances across.

They cut their names and gang-symbols into the rock, and the date. One of the boys opened a tin of petroleum jelly and lit it under a snow-filled pot; after they drank tea and ate dehydrated stew, they lay on their backs, looking straight up at Shining Sister.

"This is the closest anybody has ever gotten to

her," a girl said, putting her binoculars to her eyes and staring at the pale silver globe. "I can see some of the little islands along the Horizon Zone. I wonder what the other side's like. Do you suppose there's any land on the other side?"

"Very likely," Dirven Kalgravno, the party-leader, said. "She and our planet were both parts of a big planet beyond the orbit of Varri, that was broken up when the Red One entered our system, according to Dibbilo Stonyo. The chemical compositions of our planet and Shining Sister must be pretty much the same, so the surface conditions are probably pretty similar. Except, of course, that Shining Sister seems to have a surplus of water. But I'd say there's a good chance that most of the other side is dry land. Those islands must correspond to our Rim Country mountains."

"Why would that be?"

"Well, Dibbilo's theory of how gravitic attraction works shows that the water on Shining Sister would bunch up on the side of the planet attracted by us. And, since Shining Sister always keeps the same side turned toward us, the other side would always have less water. So it all depends on the depth of the planet-ocean. If it is as we think it is, then there must be a fair amount of land on the far side."

"But we'll never really know, will we?" the girl asked.

Dirven shook his head. "No. Shining Sister will always keep that side turned toward us. If there are people on the other side, they may not even know we exist."

"But why do you think we'll never know?" one

of the boys, Kartho Alvarrarro, spoke up. "Halli
Zarrono got her glider off the ground with a charge
of ordinary rifle-powder. One of these days, somebody will invent a special rocket explosive that will
lift some kind of glider free of gravitation, and
then—"

"It's theoretically possible," Vandro Kalgravno,
the other instructor, said, rummaging under his fur
coveralls for a pressed-food ration bar. "But
there's one great problem that we cannot, at the
present time, overcome."

Dirven turned to his fellow instructor. "One
problem?" he asked. "I see a *toulth*-load of problems. The acceleration of a vehicle shot into space
might crush the passengers. In space there is no air;
a space-glider would have to carry its own air supply. Steering a glider in space would take new
methods, since there's no air to work against. And
those are just the problems that come to mind
without trying. What is this overwhelming single
problem?"

"You've just said it," Vandro said. "The sheer
magnitude of the undertaking. All of the things
you have mentioned, and any others you can think
of, *can* be solved. But think of the planning, the
materials needed, the different gangs that would
have to work together. Probably hundreds of gangs
before the project succeeded. How would anybody
be able to organize such a thing? How would anybody be able to trade for everything that would be
needed?"

Dirvan shook his head. "I don't know."

To be an efficient trading medium, money must

either be something which compresses enormous worth into small bulk and weight, or it must be something generally accepted as redeemable in valuable commodities, or it must be guaranteed by a private group of known wealth and honesty, or a government of such power as to make it valuable by fiat.

There was nothing of such value to a Hetairan that a few pounds of it were worth, say, a steamboat-load of grain or a trainload of steel. There were warehouse certificates, showing that the bearer had in storage so much grain or hides or whiskey or steel, but over a hundred gangs in and around Arrowwood Valley had been impoverished in 267, when a steamboat loaded with blasting-paste had blown up at the dock of Balsambo Town, destroying the warehouses and the merchandise for which they held script. And there was nothing on Hetaira with any of the powers and attributes of a central government; the mere idea of any government mechanism outside of the gang was alien to the Hetairan mind.

Not that the existence of any organization larger than the gang was, any longer, inconceivable. There had been many activities requiring the close cooperation of several gangs, and combinations had been formed to carry on many undertakings. There was the Rendezvous Combine, dating back to the Sixth Century Before the Railroad, for the purpose of exchanging and preserving scientific and technological information. It had been the Rendezvous Combine which had made possible the general use of breech-loading firearms by setting standards for chamber dimensions and barrel

width to which all gunmaking and cartridge-manu-
facturing gangs had conformed. After that success,
they had established screw-thread standards, and
had taken the old, inexact and varying linear mea-
sure, the lance-length, and set up a standard lance,
divisible into hundred-thousandths.

There were the Music Combines, and the Rifle
and Revolver combine, which now set standards
for manufacturing gangs and held annual matches,
and the Climbers' Combine. Perhaps most successful was the Railroad Combine, which insured
uniform track gauges, set standards for load limits
and wheel-and-axle construction and track grades
and curves, traced cars which had been shunted
from one road to another, and handled matters of
inter-road fares and freight-bill tolls. There were
even local protection combines, an early example
of which was the force which had been raised at the
time of the Thurkka invasion.

So Hetaira was not unready for the proposal of
Kartho Alvararro when he called the meeting at
Stockade Point, overlooking Timber Lake, in 307.

Singly and in groups, they came into the big
gathering-room of the Alvararro gang-house, shaking hands with Kartho as they entered. Among
them were some of the most important people in
the Central Mountain country—Taldo Kunninzo,
the chairman of the board of advisors of the Telegraph Gangs Combine; Brammo Linzartho and
Feerk Evarro, of the Railroad Combine; Reeda
Sambro, of the Munitions Combine; and Urlik
Slidertho, head advisor of the Slidertho Weaving
Gang.

Lyssa Grassano, the advisor of advisors of the Grassano Gang, stopped short, halfway to her host, on seeing Dwallo Vallado already in the room. She lowered her glance to the Vallado advisor's belt to make sure that he, too, had divested himself of his hand-weapon. The Grassanos and the Vallados were currently feuding about a rich ore-field inside the Short Circle Line, in the mountains.

They all sat at the long table, but when the toast of friendship was drunk, the Vallado and Grassano representatives ostentatiously looked in opposite directions. Then Kartho Alvararro tapped on the rim of his glass with his gold fountain pen.

"Ladies and gentlemen," he began. "Combine advisors, and gang representatives and advisors, I welcome you each to Timber Lake. You all have a pretty good idea of what I want to propose, since I outlined it as well as possible in the letters inviting you here. And I assume you're all interested, or, at least, curious, or you wouldn't have come. To put it briefly, I propose to set up, with your cooperation, a system of exchange that will partly supplant the present barter-system, and will avoid or eliminate many of its problems. Are there any comments or suggestions from anyone before we get down to the in-depth dissection of the idea?"

"Well, *something* is certainly needed," Taldo Kunninzo said. "The Telegraph Combine prefers to take copper in exchange for sending a message, and we've worked out a regular scale of rates in copper, and a changing scale of values against copper for things like grain, that vary in worth from season to season, or coal, that vary in worth from

location to location. But, of course, we cannot refuse to send a message if someone has something
besides copper or the regular-scale items to barter.
Some of the stuff we accumulate! And we never
know, from one time to the next, what we're going
to have to give some construction-gang for string-
ing a new line, or how to make an honest and
equitable division of the profits each year."

"We can't ever seem to get any kind of a reasonable division of the profits, either," Lyssa
Grassano said. "There's always someone who's left
unhappy. And so much skill is needed by the
gang's traders, to know the value of every possible
barter-item relative to every other item, that an un-
skillful trader can cost the gang on every trans-
action that's the least bit out of the ordinary; or,
what's worse, inadvertantly cheat the customer.
Maybe this business of trading goods for goods
was all right a thousand years ago, when the gangs
were little and everybody lived in the same house
or the same village; and at the beginning it's certainly the most natural way. But it certainly does
get complex if you keep at it long enough. How are
you going to take two thousand people, all working at different jobs, and give everybody what they
want out of fifty carloads of grain and five hundred
bales of hides and a steamboat-load of lumber?"

"And suppose somebody halfway around the
mountains needs a shipment of structural steel, or
rails, and all he has to trade for it is grain, and you
already have grain running out of your ears as it is,
and what you want is electrical fittings and
ceramics and small-arms ammo?" Dwallo Vallado
threw in.

"Well, if a Vallado and a Grassano think it's a good idea, I, for one, won't argue," a representative of a coal-mining and coke-burning combine laughed. "I do business with both of them. They know what they're talking about, and *I* know what they're talking about."

"Kartho, suppose you explain your scheme," one of the railroad advisors said. "It is evident that some way of handling the transfer of goods must be found that is an improvement on the one in use, but you're going to have to show us how your system is anything better than one of those old warehouse-script schemes. That's a good idea in principle, too; but since the Balsambo blowup, everybody's been afraid to have anything to do with warehouse script."

"The warehouse script system wouldn't solve the problem even if the warehouses didn't blow up," Kartho said. "A receipt for a bale of hides or a bin of grain still represents only the receipted object; it won't do you any good if what you want is a box of cartridges. You'd still have to find someone with the cartridges who happens to need grain."

"How is your system better?" Dwallo Vallado asked.

"I propose to have a trading combine, which will include everybody here and as many more gangs as we can get to join. The combine will issue script, but it won't be for a specific object like a bale of hides; it will be for some arbitrarily agreed upon unit of value. These will be some kind of special certificates that can be used to trade for anything within the combine. And, since the combine will be so big and powerful, most gangs outside the combine, even if they don't come in, should be willing to take the certificates in trade. They'll be assured that whatever they need from within the combine can be traded for these certificates whenever they wish to use them. People with small items to trade, who wish to get a big item, like someone who makes *rogel*-leather belts and needs to get a stamping machine, can save up the certificates until they have enough to trade for the machine."

"It sounds good," an advisor from a farming gang said. "That way, if you have a boatload of grain, you won't have to wait around for somebody who wants it and has just what you want, or work out one of those complex around-the-corner-and-under-the-hedge deals, where fifteen people criss-cross receipts until everyone is happy. You could just trade your goods for the certificates, and then use them for whatever you wanted."

"That's the idea," Kartho agreed.

"Well now, wait a minute," Urlik Slidertho objected. "This idea of having something that can be traded for anything sounds fine, but how are you going to set the value of your certificates? Look, we make fifty different kinds of cloth. Each one's of a different weave, with different yarns, and has a different value. What's your standard going to be?"

"Grain," somebody suggested. "Everybody has to eat. Say a cubic tenth-lance of grain—"

"Grain's never worth the same from one year to the next!" someone yelled out. "I should know, I deal in it!"

"Lead!" Reeda Sambro piped up. "There isn't a man, woman, or child who doesn't carry a gun, and a gun's no use without bullets."

"A unit of value will have to be decided upon," Kartho Alvararro said. "We'll find one that we can all mutually agree on. It doesn't really matter what it is, you see; as long as it's the same for each certificate, any place within the combine territory, at any time. There are things to be said for a number of possible standards. It might be a good idea, for example, to use grain. If we made it the standard of value, that in itself might have a stabilizing effect on the trading of grain. But, on the other hand, if it doesn't, then the fluctuating value of grain would affect the worth of the certificates in a way that people might find unacceptable."

"We could use a sort of 'box of commodities,' " one of the farmers suggested. "Say we pick out the ten or twenty most important commodities and take an average of their relative values for the last ten years, and work out some kind of common denominator. Then everyone can figure out the value of his own goods or services accordingly; the prices of other commodities will naturally adjust themselves according to demand."

"That sounds more complex than the system we're using," Reeda Sambro called out, "I would have thought it impossible!"

"There's another, completely separate problem," Dwallo Vallado said. "When these certificates are in use, what's to stop some unscrupulous person—or gang—from imitating them? At least with a bale of hides, you have the bale of hides. With an imitation certificate, what would you have?"

"That is a very real problem," Kartho Alvararro admitted.

"We'd have to make the certificates on some kind of fancy paper—special paper that nobody else could get hold of," Lyssa Grassano suggested. "And make them as intricate as possible; all over little curlicues, pictures by master engravers, very hard to duplicate. And make only one set of plates to print them, and keep them under reliable guard."

"We could organize a special gang to go after imitators," Taldo Kunnizo, the Telegraph Gangs Combine man said. "Hunt down the makers of false certificates and kill them. If this special gang is efficient, it should discourage the practice."

"If the gang is efficient enough," Kartho commented, "it will eliminate the practice entirely."

"Your notion is good, Lyssa," Dwallo Vallado said. "If we add a few little hidden mistakes in the engraving, things that only those who regularly handle the script would notice, it might help."

Kartho Alvararro noted that the representatives of the two feuding steel-gangs seemed to have put aside their shoot-on-sight enmity, and both seemed enthusiastically in favor of the proposal. "Do you two think that you can work on that idea together without jumping at each other's throats over the Painted Hills business?" he asked. "Lyssa, I know you're good with drafting tools, you can work up a design, with Dwallo to help you."

"You know, if we can make a go of this scheme, our gangs could probably get together on the Painted Hills mines. There's enough ore there for both of us, if we could figure out some fair way to divide it."

"Well, how would this Trading Combine support itself?" somebody asked. "And how about possible disasters, like the cattle-plague of 274, or the Balsambo explosion? Wouldn't something like that still put the Combine out of business?"

"To the first question," Kartho said, "the Combine will take a percentage, like a milling or distilling gang takes a percentage of the grain. It can be a very small percentage. As to the second, destruction of any kind of product will not affect the value of the script, because it will carry its own value when it trades for the products. Any script destroyed by fire or flood can be replaced if the holder can prove the destruction. We do have to guard against theft, but that is true of any valuable goods. I think we'll probably have to have a few special strong-rooms in different areas, and keep them well guarded. Small losses, even ones that would be major to any one gang, will simply even themselves out.

"Look, Feerk; you remember reading about how the old Hoona River Railroad was put out of business in 65, when their only two locomotives and thirty of their cars were wrecked in a collision? Well, what would happen if somebody had a wreck like that now?"

Feerk considered. "If they belonged to the Railroad Combine," he said, "they'd borrow an engine here and an engine there, and cars from all around, and the combine would get them new rolling stock as soon as possible, and let them trade for it as soon as they were able. A thing like that wouldn't interrupt service for more than a sleep-period or two. And besides, most of the railroad gangs have enough of a reserve—" He stopped. "I think I see

what you're getting at. A combine like you're prop-
osing would be too big to be hurt by any local dis-
aster; Skystabber's too big to be knocked down
with a cannon."

The meeting continued, with only short interrup-
tions for food and rest, while the sun crawled thirty degrees across the sky. They hammered out
compromises, raised and disposed of objections,
convinced each other that the idea would, indeed,
work. Finally Brammo Lazanthro rose to his feet.
"Ladies and gentlemen, we've been at this for the
last two sleep-periods—and none of us have taken
much time out to do the sleeping. I think we have
the basic idea straight in our minds. Let's take a
vote on it now, as to whether or not we want to
commit our gangs and combines to the scheme. After that we can work out the little details. Personally, I'm getting sleepy, and I wouldn't mind having a decent meal instead of arguing with a cup of
tea in one hand and a meat-roll pastry in the other."

"Yes, let's vote already," Reeda Sambro, the advisor of the Munitions Combine agreed. "Here,
this will do!"

She was sitting on Kartho Alvararro's right. She
picked up a sheet of paper, wrote on it, and passed
it to the man on her right. When the paper had
gone once around the table, it ended at Kartho.

He looked at it and smiled. "Well, out of forty-
two of you, everybody has voted for the new combine but Ranna Satallano, who thinks the plan
isn't fully enough developed to vote on yet, and
Bordo Rakkajoro, who thinks such a combine
would subject the members to compulsion which

might end up infringing upon their individual rights. I take it, then, that the rest of you speak for your gangs or combines, and will bring them into the Trading Combine. Ranna, will you go along with the majority?"

The representative of the Chemicals Combine shrugged. "I only thought we ought to work it out in detail before we positively adopt it," she said, "but we can finish it from the inside as easily as from the outside. So, if the rest of you are determined to start the Combine here and now, then my group is in."

"You, Bordo?"

"It's going to mean that this Trading Combine will get too much power," Bordo Rakkajoro, who represented a combine of traders from the other side of the Central Mountains, said. "But, if my crowd doesn't join, the rest of you just might squeeze us out of business. All right, my combine's in—under protest!"

"You won't regret it, Bordo. And I suggest that we put you to the task of drawing up a set of rules for us that will prevent that from happening. Now, let's all get some sleep. After we're all awake we can get down to the business of organizing this."

Chairs scraped as the conference broke up. Dwallo Vallado and Lyssa Grassano were going out of the room arm in arm; if their new friendship rubbed off on their two gangs, the meeting would have been worthwhile for that alone. Reeda Sambro fell into step with Kartho as they went out.

"Where did you get this idea from, anyhow, Kartho?" she asked.

"On top of Skystabber," he told her seriously.

He related the conversation among the victorious climbers as they rested at the summit, that time thirty years ago. "I've always wanted to see the other side of Shining Sister. I probably shan't live long enough to, but I'm going to do what I can toward starting the process. That was why I organized a gang to get into the aircraft business, back when the only aircraft were rocket-assisted gliders, and everyone thought I had eaten too much fungus, and was seeing that-which-was-not."

They stepped out onto the veranda and looked up at their world's companion-planet.

"Another thing more immediate," he continued. "My gang is working on a new engine; one that burns a volatile fluid refined from petroleum. It works like the present coal-gas engines, but has more power. Before we can get it into general use, though, we'll have to have a large and dependable fuel supply. There isn't enough petroleum in the Central Mountains, but it's fairly sloshing around a few hundred lance-lengths under the ground everywhere in the Rim Country. If we can get a railroad out there, we'll have thousands of aircraft flying all over the planet in the next ten years."

At first the world was cautious in accepting the new trading certificates, but by the middle of the Fourth Century, when Kartho Alvararro was dead and Reeda Sambro was an old woman, they had so revolutionized the economy of Hetaira that the barter system, in use for so many thousands of years, had just about faded away. It seemed fantastically remote, even to those old enough to remember having done business under it. Heretofore, technological progress had been a slow, steady push; now it became a torrent after the breaking of an ice-gorge.

By the Year of the Railroad 416, there were railroads across the plains to the Rim Country, and a four-track line completely circling the planet along the Horizon Zone, and lines into the Outer Hemisphere clear to the Central Sea. There was no place left on the planet to which motor-truck caravans or huge transport and passenger airplanes did not go. The telegraph had been superceded by the telephone, and the telephone would have been generally superceded by the radio except that Hetaira, like Thalassa, possessed only the slightest trace of an ionosphere. Radio waves had nothing to bounce off of, and headed in straight lines to outer space.

Line-of-sight broadcasting was possible, and in some areas chains of relay stations were set up on mountain tops. There was a powerful station on the very summit of Skystabber, reached by a series of cable-lifts that were of themselves an engineering project of the first magnitude. There was also an observatory there, and a great telescope was kept aimed at Shining Sister, even though all that could be seen was the unbroken expanse of the Ocean Sea, the few small islands of the Horizon Zone, and an occasional cloud bank.

Then, in the year 416, a black smudge was seen to obscure one group of islands. It was not a cloud, and through it the observers were sure they could make out glimpses of orange flame. At first it was supposed that a volcano had broken into activity, but when the smoke cleared, in less than one waking-period, there was no discernable alteration in the shape of the islands.

This was the first date which could be fixed in both Hetairan and Thalassan history; it was the day of the burning of the Zabashan fishing-fleet by the ships of Gir-Zashon.

Chapter Ten

However scrupulously the historian may shun value-judgments, the Thalassan Fish Oil War can only be characterized as a senseless and barbarous folly. The Ocean Sea was so vast, and its marine life so prolific, that the whole population of Thalassa might have exploited its resources for all eternity without having occasion for conflict. The war began without legitimate reason or necessity, and it ended in the ruin of every participant. Only the kingdoms and city-states of Dudak remained neutral, carrying on trade with both Gir-Zashon and Thurv, and with the Sabashan-Vashturan-Nimshan-Gvardan allies.

The war ended in the year 1950 of the Tisséan Era, with the defeat of Gir-Zashonan and Thurv. The whole of Thurv was overrun and conquered by Vashturan and Gvardan armies; several powerful Gir-Zashonan fleets were destroyed in naval battles on the Central Sea; two of the three semi-autonomous states of Gir-Zashon became embroiled in a civil war growing out of mutual accusations of cowardice and treachery. The war itself, begun without formal declaration, ended without formal peace. Everybody was tired of it; even the nominal victors were glad to see its end. The credit for finally halting the war goes to the then Successor of Puzzá, and Interpreter of The Books of Tissé, Avaraff XVI, who finally managed to get an agreement from all parties; negotiating with the states of Gir-Zashon and Thurv through one Horv-Haddrov, a Gir-Zashonan general who had been taken prisoner several years before and converted to the Puzzán creed at Tullon.

Although the peace obviously saved the Gir-Zashonan states from extinction, there was bitter dissatisfaction within Gir-Zashon. All three of the semi-autonomous governments were overthrown, the people accusing them of having stabbed the armies and fleets of Gir-Zashon in the back. Horv-Haddrov, returning to Karkasha, was dragged from the rostrum while attempting to explain the terms of the peace and lynched with shocking brutality. Other members of the peace party, especially the clergy of Puzzánism, were the victims of savage pogroms. In the century which followed, at least fifty governments were toppled from power in the three states of Gir-Zashon; their political backgrounds ranging from absolute monarchy to total anarchy.

It was at Karkasha, near the mid-mark of this century of disorder, that Dov-Soglov wrote his brief thesis, *The Organic State.* Dov-Soglov was no superstitious and subliterate Tissé, dictating his random thoughts over a pot of beer to a drinking-crony while he pegged the soles of peasants' sandals. His portraits, admittedly idealized, show a serious and intelligent face, with much darker head-

down than was usual among the Hoz-Hozgaz race,
and the close-set eyes, small ears, and pointed nose
of the mountain people of the interior. He was for
some time a student in one of the secular universities at Karkasha, and, simultaneously, held some
minor clerical post in one of the kaleidoscopically-
shifting governments of the period. His studies
seem to have been in the field of anatomy and what
passed, in his culture, for biology.

The state, according to his book, was analogous
to a living organism, and obeyed laws parallel to
the laws of organic growth and evolution. Each individual was therefore a part of the organism, and
could have no function or duty save the service of
the organism-as-a-whole. Not "no *higher* duty"
than service to the state, but no other duty at all.
Individualism was a species of social cancer. As the
body is directed by a central nervous system, the
state must be directed by a governing elite, to
whom the "body-cells" must give absolute obedience for their own good.

Dov-Soglov lived only eight years after the publication of his book, but in that time he saw it become a subject of hot discussion all over the planet.
The hierarchy of Puzzán Tisséism and the
Zaithuan Congregations outdid one another in de-
nouncing it; the latter because it was revolting to
their individualistic principles, and the former because it proposed a rival authoritarianism too
much like their own. Absolute monarchs and dictators approved it—with much suspicion and with
reservations—and quoted or misquoted from it to
support their authority. The workers and peasants,
slave and free, hailed it as a promise of equality

and fraternity for all. Workers and peasants tend
to be out of touch with their own best interests.
And adventurers saw in it a ladder to power.

Within twenty years of Dov-Soglov's death,
there was a strong, if clandestine, Organicist move-
ment on every continent around the Central Sea.
Everywhere its existence was illegal and secret, its
advocates slinking among the poor and oppressed
with glowing promises of freedom and prosperity
for all. There were governments, even formally
democratic republics, which adopted parts of Dov-
Soglov's political gospel and grasped more and
more authority in the name of such meaningless
abstractions as "the common welfare," or "the
greatest good for the greatest number." Whenever
possible, Organicists managed to infiltrate as many
of their supporters as possible into such governments. This even happened in states which looked
for spiritual guidance to the Puzzán Creed.

The end of the Fish Oil War had brought peace,
but not prosperity to Thalassa. With the exception
of the Confederacy of Dudak, which had stayed
out of it, every nation around the Central Sea
either stood on the crumbling edge of bankruptcy,
or had gathered skirt in hand and leapt headlong
over it. The introduction of new weapons had
forced all of them into rearmament programs far
beyond their financial or technological capacities.
The fishing fleets were devastated; merchant ships,
the red corpuscles of trade, were mostly sunk or
burned in port. Blockades and commerce-raiding
had forced every continent into a shabby self-suffi-
ciency based on a make-do or do-without
philosophy. Everybody was poor, and almost ev-

erybody went to bed hungry nine times out of ten.

Gir-Zashon was the first to go completely Organicist. Conditions there were worse than on any other continent, with the exception of Thurv, still occupied after a century by Zabashan troops. The last of a long series of progressively weaker governments could no longer suppress the hungry rioters, and collapsed into a shambles of blood and destruction. The Organicists, organized, disciplined, armed with secretly accumulated stores of weapons and ammunition, and reenforced by comrades from overseas, waited until the whole continent was in anarchy and then took over in a series of almost bloodless coups. The bloodshed would come later.

Hetairan history had not been without its bloody pages. There had been no national wars, for there were no nations; but as gangs grew larger, conflicts between them approached the ferocity and intensity of wars. There had been the Sugar Valley Massacre; people still talked of the wiping out of the Halzorros and their bandit mercenaries. There had been fights between migratory labor-gangs. There had been the Painted Hills War, between the Vallados and the Grassanos, which ended after the first Timber Lake Conference as a result of the friendship and collaboration between Dwallo Vallado and Lyssa Grassano. This collaboration may have resulted in more than that—it was rumored that Dwallo may have been the father of Lyssa's next child. This was somewhat shocking. Liaisons with wanderers were acceptable, but with that one exception, sex outside of the gang was discouraged by an ancient, unspoken taboo. After all, the gang had to raise the offspring of any such liaison. The rumor itself was regarded as almost indecent, the only form of indecency existing in any Hetairan language, although the mere act of attempting to trace the paternity of a child was, in itself, regarded as in extremely poor taste.

In one way the Trading Combine was a force for peace: gang wars were definitely bad for business. When, however, such clashes could not be averted, they were apt to be far more extensive, sanguinary, and destructive, as inter-gang connections grew. In the Fifth Century there was an oil-war in the Rim Country which lasted for five years; both sides used armored trucks and dropped bombs of blasting-paste from transport planes. The Trading Combine tried to stop it by cutting off credit to the two warring oil-gangs, but this only hurt business even more, and both gangs were able to borrow from independant banking groups. It proved, at least, that the Trading Combine was not the all-powerful monster that so many small gangs had feared.

No gang or combine, however, was ever able to so completely dominate any geographical area as to resemble, even remotely, a national state; and such a thing as government was an idea that never developed. Armed individuals protected themselves. Hetairans of good will were always willing to band together to put down brigandage. Roads were built out of common need, and paid for by the users. Fire protection was supplied by a gang, and paid for like an insurance policy. Police protection could be supplied the same way, if anyone felt the need.

Hetaira was a world of order in the absence of law; if violence between individuals was common, and violence between gangs possible, at least the greater violence that was possible between nations was completely unknown. The individual's rifle or revolver was less of a burden to him than a nation's armies and air-fleets would have been, and far less of a danger to his neighbors. There was very little incentive for an arms-race.

The day after the smoke-smudge was observed on Shining Sister, the newspapers all over the planet carried the story; and for years to come they were filled with the continuing controversy as to just what this signified. There had never, since the establishment of the observatory on Skystabber, been any trace of volcanic activity on Shining Sister. While this proved nothing, it gave support to the view that the smoke was the result of some artificial process caused by intelligent beings.

The radio station began beaming signals toward the other planet. They went unanswered for the excellent reason that there was not, on Thalassa, at that time, a single radio to receive them or reply. A closer watch was kept through the big telescope. Occasionally smaller smudges were detected on the open water. Some optimists were of the firm opinion that these were signal-fires, but the prevalent— and correct—opinion was that these were burning ships. One scientists approached absolute truth when he opined that it was probably the sign of a great gang-war in progress.

The interest in Shining Sister was powerful and universal, deeply involving the emotions of everybody. For over a thousand years it had been known that she was a duplicate world, formed, along with their own, from the wreckage of a single planet in a great stellar cataclysm. In the Hetairan social organization the family, as such, was non-existant. The only blood relationship commonly recognized was that of mother and child, and between children of the same mother. The binary planetary system they were a part of was, perhaps inevitably, conceived of as—in poetic terms—the two children of a single mother, who gave her life in their birth.

For thousands of years they had looked toward the unmoving globe in the sky, first with wonder, then as a reliable landmark, and finally, when their astronomers established the relationship, with familial love. And now it seemed strongly probable that Shining Sister had children with whom they could communicate.

An attitude of something less—or something more—than logic, perhaps? Though extremely logical, the Hetairan was not exclusively logical. About some things he could be passionately emotional. And so, compelled by the two poles of logic and emotion, the Shining Sister Combine was formed by the scientists of the Rendezvous Combine, and, almost immediately, heavily subscribed by the general public.

The six who sat in the ornate-shabby room were variously clad. Yev-Lorov, paring an apple-like fruit with his knife, wore the leather smock of a carpenter, but there was a heavy pistol thrust through the loop in which a carpenter usually carried his square, a powder-flask in one side pocket and a book in the other. Tav-Jarkthov and Olv-Yakkov wore military uniforms, one of cavalry and the other of the Brigade of Naval Infantry; they were playing cards at one end of the table. Thav-Thabov, in the sleeveless jerkin of a merchant's clerk, had one of his pistols apart and was cleaning it. Rav-Razkov, in his student's gown, with an artillery private's carbine slung from his shoulder, was peering at the titles of the books on the shelves across the room. And Zov-Zolkov lounged, seemingly asleep, in the armchair once occupied by the High Courts judge whose private chamber this room had been; except for the tip of one ear, which would twitch occasionally, he was utterly motionless.

The group shared two things in common: they each had a white armband bearing, in black, a cubist humanoid figure, stylized to the point of inhumanity; and they each had the bitter, hate-filled, utterly humorless expression of the complete fanatic.

"Cattle!" Thav-Thabov said contemptuously. "They riot for bread—and they begin by destroying the bakeries!"

"'And on the farm,'" Raz-Razkov quoted, "'there are the cattle, and the herdsmen, and there are those who tell the herdsmen where to drive the cattle, and what to feed them, and which are to be milked, and which bred, and which slaughtered.'"

"You can quote the Citizen-Originator about anything at all," Yev-Lorov admired. "Me, I have to carry *The Organic State* in my pocket, but you have it all in your head."

"If you'd spent five years in prison as I did," Raz-Razkov said, "you'd know it all by heart, too."

There was a sound outside the door; the faint rattle of a musket-sling, as the sentinel brought his weapon to the ready. Only the apparently somnolent Zov-Zolkov heard it; his hand went to the pistol inside his jacket, and then he relaxed as the door opened and a man in the trousers of a workman, the coat of an infantry captain, and a steel helmet, entered.

"Obedience, Citizen First Controller," he greeted Zov-Zolkov. "All the gates of the city are in our hands. Citizen-Lieutenant Niv-Hazrov's force controls the warehouse district, and Citizen-Captain Yav-Novrov sends word from the rural districts that the seizure of grain and meat-animals is progressing, and what little resistance he had encountered has been dealt with according to The Words of Instruction."

Zov-Zolkov smiled—not a pleasant smile. "Excellent, Citizen. Have you notified Citizen Trav-Vasov? Then do so at once; he has his instructions."

"Obedient to your will, Citizen First Controller!" The messenger turned and went out, closing the door behind him.

"The cattle will be lowing to be fed, soon," Zov-Zolkov said. "The herdsmen have been told under what conditions to feed them . . . Citizens, we will now proceed to construct the Organic State."

The construction was neither swift nor nice. Peasants and workers who had gulped the doctrines of Dov-Soglov whole, without pausing to savor the taste or texture, which is to say without examining the details or understanding just what their position in the Organic hierarchy was to be, had to be made to understand that they were cattle on the farm of Zov-Zolkov; bone-cells and muscle-cells in the body of the State, of which the Party was the brain and Zov-Zolkov the First Controller. The understanding usually came painfully. There were certain brain-cells, too, which had to be excised when they began disagreeing among themselves. Yav-Lorov was one of these; he was put on trial for contra-organicism, convicted without dissent, and brained with an iron mace. Execution by shooting was a useless expenditure of ammunition, and therefore a criminal waste of the resources of the State. His crime appears to have been disagreement with the Citizen First Controller about agrarian policy, again a matter of conservation of the resources of the State.

The resources of the State were the first concern of all; they had to be husbanded and multiplied. Every one of the humanoid resources—the body-cells, in the Citizen-Originator's metaphor—must perform precisely as much work as possible; they must be asked for no more, and they must deliver not one tap less. They must eat and wear and use what was barely necessary for the work they must do. They must reproduce themselves with the same machine-like efficiency with which they produced food and clothing and tools and weapons. After all, their children would be, in a very real sense, the tools and weapons of the State.

They were shifted from job to job, from place to

place, from mate to mate, at the dictates of the First Controller and the Board of Deputy Control and the Board of Planning. They owned nothing, not even themselves. It must be said that Zov-Zolkov and his Deputy-Controllers drove themselves as hard as they drove the "body-cells," but that merely made the enslavement of Gir-Zashon complete.

In the earlier phases of the Organic State, technological advancement had top priority. Dov-Soglov, when his thinking had not been distorted by too-rigid adherence to anatomical analogies, had been a keen student of political history. He had realized that from the days of the First Sea Empire on Gvarda, the limiting factor upon the growth and survival of every state had been its level of technology, and he had postulated that the state can only grow numerically and geographically to the extent that it has the tools for supplying its subjects, communicating with the edges of its domain, and waging successful war upon its enemies. With this dictum Zov-Zolkov agreed wholeheartedly, not only because it would have been unthinkable for him not to do so, but because, if Dov-Soglov had not said so, he would have thought of it himself.

He established research and development centers; he selected the most intelligent "body-cells" and trained them to be "brain-cells"; he collected books on every scientific subject from all around the Central Sea; he imported scientists and technicians from every country on the globe and devised methods to encourage them to work for the State. Steam-turbine engines were improved, and gas-turbine engines designed. Electricity, long a classroom demonstration-toy in other lands, was studied and applied to industry and communication; electric lighting and power and the telephone were developed, and eventually the principles of radio were discovered.

Raz-Razkov was Zov-Zolkov's designated successor; after fifteen years as Second-Controller, he began to observe that the Citizen First Controller was growing absent-minded. If the director of the State Brain was beginning to fail, it was Rav-Razkov's clear Organicist duty to amputate him. The amputation was performed with a pinch of fast-acting poison in Citizen Zov-Zolkov's breakfast porridge; thereafter Rav-Razkov was Citizen First Controller.

The Organic State, in Raz-Razkov's hitherto scrupulously private opinion, had become too static. The body should grow; growth was an inescapable function of organic survival. The growing-pains began to be felt immediately on the neighboring continent of Thurv, still occupied by Zabashan troops. An intense infiltration of Organicist agents was carried on; incidents of conflict between Thurvans and Zabashan soldiers were provoked; atrocity-stories were manufactured and circulated wholesale; old songs and stories of Thurvan nationalism were rummaged out of the rag-bag of the past.

The Thurvan revolution, when it came, was organized and led from the start by Organicists; the Thurvan nationalists had been convinced that the Organic State was only interested in establishing a friendly independent government on Thurv. A series of apparently spontaneous riots and uprisings was engineered, there were a number of sensational assassinations, and the Thurvan Civil War was off to a galloping start.

Naturally, as soon as the Zabashans on Thurv were all either massacred or expelled, the Organicists took over; the pattern of their conquest of Gir-Zashon was repeated in detail, and Thurv became the second member of what was now being called the World Organic State. The orders, of course, came from Karkasha, and were transmitted through the "herdsmen" to the "cattle" in heavily Gir-Zashonan accents.

Even before the amputation of the former First Controller, a project had been forming in Rav-Razkov's mind. Now that he was in absolute and unquestioned authority, he began to give it his full attention.

Since the institution of the Organic State, in 2052, there had existed between it and the Puzzán version of Tisséism a mutually implacable hostility. "Religion," Dov-Soglov had written, "is a dangerous hypnotic. It deadens the body-cells and prevents their obedience to the brain; it numbs the brain-cells and interferes with their control of the body." However, Rav-Razkov considered, even the most dangerous drugs have their uses; no surgeon would care to be without certain hypnotics and anaesthetics, for example. And he had noticed that the organism of Puzzáism had been functioning quite efficiently for a long time; its body-cells, the laity, were entirely submissive to the hierarchial brain-cells. If, in some way, the Organic State could only get control of this marvelous engine of intellectual domination . . .

He established a select group of young, competent, aggressive "brain-cells" and put them to con-
ducting an intensive study of Puzzán Tisséism.
The secret police discovered a number of under-
ground Puzzán congregations on Gir-Zashon,
and were even aware of the identity of a Puzzán
archpriest, a Nimshan named Varthad, who was
hiding at a farming-center along the coast, and
who was in regular communication with the hierarchy at Tullon. Rav-Razkov ordered the police to
pick up this archpriest and bring him in.

The prelate, when he was arrested, resigned himself to being brained with the state amputation
mace, and took what solace he could from the
martyr's crown that would be his in the Memory of
Vran. Instead, he was conveyed in a fast car to
Karkasha and taken directly to the private cham-
bers of Rav-Razkov, where he was courteously in-
vited to sit, and offered wine. Rav-Razkov even
performed the supreme courtesy to his guest of
drinking first from the bottle.

"Citizen Archpriest," the First Controller said,
"I have to confess to you; I have been in grievous
error."

Archpriest Varshad started; these were the ritual
words of a penitent. The unorthodox mode of ad-
dress, however, warned him to move cautiously; a
warning that was echoed and inforced by every
item of his surroundings.

"Brother First Controller, it is my duty to coun-
sel all those who find themselves in error," he replied. "If you will tell me—"

"The writings of the Citizen Originator, Dov-

Soglov, were the beginning, not the end, of the Organic State," Rav-Razkov said. "Man is indeed a body, and the State must govern and direct its citizens as the brain directs the body. But man is also a soul, and the State is a part of the Mind of Vran, as the individual is a part of the State. To govern the soul, there must be religion, and as there must be agreement between the body and the soul, so must there be agreement between the State and the religion."

"But the soul is more than the body, Brother First Controller," Varthad reminded him timidly. "It is eternal in the Memory of Vran, and the body perishes."

"True," Rav-Razkov agreed. "So the State must be constructed according to religious principles . . . the principles of the true religion," he added with feeling.

Varthad caught his breath. Was it possible, he wondered, that a miracle had opened the heart of this wicked—no, this spiritually blind—man?

"As I am the First Controller of the State, I must be instructed in the principles of your religion, Citizen Archpriest. If you will stay here, with me—"

So Varthad was lodged in an apartment in the great building, the former palace of the Princes of Karkasha and now known as the Skull of the State; he was furnished a tailor to make his vestments, and given a dozen servants, all Puzzáns. He spent his time teaching Rav-Razkov and his henchmen, and, of course, was in constant communication with Tullón.

Rav-Razkov's only fear was that things were going too well.

The Successor of Puzzá, Avaraff XXI, was delighted with the reports which reached him from Varthad at Karkasha. His first glowing hopes of an immediate conversion to the Creed of all Organicist heathendom proved premature; Rav-Razkov was stubborn about relinquishing some of his un-Vranly errors. He did, however, proclaim freedom of worship to the followers of Puzzá, and, what was almost as good, this grant of freedom was not extended to the Zaithuan heresy; Zaithuans were persecuted with even sterner rigor.

When Rav-Razkov estimated that things had gone about as far as they should, he took his next step, the incitement of war with the Continental Republic of Zabash. Some two or three thousand Zabashan troops had escaped from Thurv after the Civil War; they had carried home with them frightening stories of the new Gir-Zashonan weapons, and of the discipline and ferocity of the "volunteers" from Gir-Zashon. The rather loosely organized government of Zabath had fallen; the new government, assuming extra-ordinary powers, had begun a frantic rearmament program, endeavoring to arm and train an army on the Gir-Zashonan pattern.

After a series of provocations and incidents intended to make Zabash appear to be the aggressor, war broke out. There were several spectacular but inconclusive naval battles, and a landing of Gir-Zashonan troops on the coast of Zabash, carefully staged to assume the appearance of a dangerous invasion. Avaraff XXI, the Successor of Puzzá, fell neatly into the trap. He sent an offer of mediation to both the Premier of the Zabashan Republic and the Citizen First Controller. Rav-Razkov accepted at once, with protestations of his deep love of peace. Premier Moganna of Zabash, a pious Puzzán, could do nothing but follow suit. The peace-conference was held at Tullon, under the auspices of the Successor of Puzzá and Interpreter of The Books of Tissé.

Rav-Razkov and the puppet First Controller of the Autonomous Organic State of Thurv, the latter a Thurvan Organicist educated at Karkasha, were all sweet conciliation. Freedom of Puzzán worship, which, to maintain the fiction of Thurvan autonomy, had not been established on that continent, was promptly decreed, and religious education of children was ordered on both Organicist continents. On Gir-Zashon and Thurv, the heretical Zaithan Confession was formally outlawed. The invasion force was withdrawn from Zabash, but in its place an army of secret agents was infiltrated into the country. There was a long dicker over indemnities, both sides magnanimously claiming to owe the most. In his ecclesiastical quality, Avariff proclaimed that there was nothing in the political principles of Organicism which conflicted with the tenets of Puzzánism or The Books of Tissé. The Organicist Party was given legal recognition in the Zabashan Republic. Rav-Razkov and his followers all announced their conversion to the creed of Puzzá.

In the years following Rav-Razkov's rise to power, the technological program instituted by Zov-Zolkov had been pushing forward rapidly. Turbojet aircraft engines were devised, and high-altitude, high-performance airplanes were developed to use them. The Organicist State possessed quite a few of them, including some specifically designed as heavy bombers, at the time of the Zabashan War. A few aircraft, mostly light fighters and reconaissance planes, had been built elsewhere. After the peace of Tullon, Rav-Razkov expanded his plane-production enormously.

In 2078, five years after the Peace of Tullon, war broke out between the Organic States of Gir-Zashon and Thurv and the Kingdoms of Dudak; ostensibly as a result of a dispute over fishing rights in the Outward Islands. The Dudakans had managed to build a few aircraft on their own, but by this time the Organic States possessed great fleets of them. They had also built large numbers of gas-turbine armored trucks, which carried cannon, rocket-launchers, and flame-projectors. Their standards blessed by Puzzán priests, the armies of Gir-Zashon and Thurv overran Dudak. Between one hot-season and the next, the whole continent was conquered, its cities blasted to rubble by Organicist aircraft.

One exception was the city of Urava, which was spared from bombardment and taken virtually intact by ground-troops. In Urava, Tissé had dictated his Books to Puzzá; the building in which he had had his shop was still claimed to be in existence, even though the city had been totally destroyed several times in the twenty intervening centuries. The Shop of the Cobbler was supposed to have been miraculously spared, and was now reverently preserved. It still contained a shoemaker's bench, rather chipped up with the passage of time, claimed to be the original. Devout pilgrims often fainted at the sight of it; all sorts of miraculous cures were reported. Little slivers of the original bench were sold to devout pilgrims at a nearby shop run by the Brothers of the Holy Order of The Books of Tissé. It was said that if all the slivers were put together, they would form a bench ten leagues long, two leagues wide, and half a league high.

That the Shop had, for so long, been in heretical hands had always been a burning sorrow to the Successors of Puzzá. Now, by the arms of the Tisséan Organic State, it was restored to the True Faith.

Raz-Razkov razed everything for blocks around the shop. Thousands of enslaved Dudakans toiled to build a shrine over it, and a huge temple of the Puzzán Creed, and a palace. Then Raz-Razkov sent a battle-fleet to Tullon to escort the Successor to the Holy City, which became both the center of Puzzán Tisséism and the capital of the World Organic State.

Two years later, an election on Zabash, marked by considerable pistol-and-truncheon campaigning, brought the Organicists into power. The conquest of Gvarda, the next year, was more a military parade than a war. Raz-Razkov now felt that his digression into Puzzán Tisséism had served its purpose. The hypnotic of religion could not be phased out, and slowly replaced with a completely secular form of Organicism.

Raz-Razkov's death came as a complete surprise to everyone, and especially Raz-Razkov himself. "It is not time," he was heard to murmur with his last breath. His funeral rites were conducted by the new Successor of Puzzá, Varthad I, who always held that his deepest satisfaction was that he, personally, had converted the Citizen First Controller to Puzzánism. He was almost as proud of the fact that it was Raz-Razkov who had introduced him to the satisfying logic and inescapable beauty of Organicism. Varthad I lived to see the two become indistinguishable. Raz-Razkov's title and position was taken by Tov-Varsor, Puzzán priest as well as a political disciple of Raz-Razkov; he assumed, on the death of Varthad, the title of Successor of Puzzá and Dov-Soglov, and Spiritual and Organic Controller. The title was eventually shortened to Successor-Controller.

There was a radio receiver at Skystabber Observatory, with its antenna directed to receive any possible signal from Shining Sister. Through the years it had been carefully maintained, its speaker kept turned up. It automatically tuned through the radio spectrum, shifting back and forth from one possible frequency to another. It produced, for almost a century and a half, an uninterrupted gabble of static, which the observatory staff quickly learned to ignore.

So, half a sun-trip after the west-to-east hot season of the year of the Railroad 556, it was some moments before anybody realized that the usual cacaphony of whistling, squealing, crackling, and buzzing had briefly been interrupted by indisputable spoken words.

Whoever was nearest the radio jumped for it, tuning back to recapture the signal and then stabbing the frequency-shift lock button. More voices were coming in, jabbering excitedly, and there were noises that sounded more like automatic-weapons fire than like any kind of static. One of the observers grabbed a telephone and began calling all the stations on the lower peaks around Skystabber. Others were yelling the news to the living-quarters. The head observer came running out of his bath, his fur white with soap-lather.

"Should we try to answer it?" a girl asked.

He listened for a minute, and then shook his head. "No, they're not trying to communicate with us. Those background noises sound like gunfire; probably a gang-fight going on. If we did manage to cut in on their conversation, we'd only mess things up for them, maybe get somebody killed."

"It certainly does sound like firing," Karna Tessaro, the Chief Analyser, said. "Mondro Salgarvo was right in his theory about the cause of that black smoke that was sighted back in 416. Gavro, do you think we can determine which part of the planet these signals are coming from?"

"We'll play with the directional antenna," Gavro Kanzalgo said, "and see what happens."

"Good," Karna said, her eyes sparkling. "If we can pinpoint the signal, or even come close, we can aim the telescope at that point on the Planet's rim. Maybe we can make out something."

"Gavro! Gavro!" one of the junior assistants called. "The head adviser of Shining Sister Combine is on the phone! Can you talk to him?"

"Of course; give me the phone! Why, this is the most wonderful thing ever! Our lovely Sister's children!" There was a hint of tears in Gavro's eyes, and his hand shook as he took the phone from the boy. "Brando, old friend! Isn't this marvelous!"

The Shining Sister Combine, relatively dormant after the excitement of a hundred and forty years before, became the center of public attention again. Fresh contributions poured in. The Skystabber Observatory bubbled with activity.

The first message to be beamed toward Shining Sister went out several sleep-periods later, after Brando Lanorgo, the head adviser of Shining Sister Combine, landed in his vertical-horizontal aircraft outside the observatory. It was cobbled together, a compromise between several conflicting notions, and consisted of a bar of music, followed by the words: "Sister's Children, we send you our love. Can you hear us?" and then a second bar of music. For the equivalent of thirty sleep-periods it was repeated. There was nothing that could be considered an answer, even by the most enthusiastic, although other messages were picked up from time to time. Then there came an unbroken radio silence from Shining Sister.

There had been some air and sea fighting in the Outward Islands during the earlier phases of the Conquest of Dudak, and some of the aircraft, equipped with radio, had reported hearing mysterious signals, of unknown origin, consisting of what sounded like harp-music mixed with unintelligible gibberish. The origin-point must have been somewhere along the line-of-sight, because of the well-known behavior of radio waves on a planet with no effective ionosphere. But no possible origin-point could be found. Eventually, after prolonged enquiry, the thick report folder was relegated to the inactive files. An archival clerk with a passion for the odd and inexplicable saved it when the seat of government was moved from

Karkasha to Urava in 2080.

In the years of peace which followed the conquest of Dudak and Gvarda and the political victory in Zabash, the technique of sea-monster hunting was improved by the introduction of aircraft-carrying hunter-ships and the use of tethered-balloons and radio for spotting and directing. Consequently, considerable radio-communication was going on among the islands and on the Ocean Sea beyond. There were scattered reports, only gradually consolidated, of mysterious signals being picked up. The brain-cell in the Fish-Oil Production Bureau who first noted the relationship between the reports did some checking first on his own. Then he flew directly to Urava from Valkor Island, where he was in charge of the refinery complex, and requested an immediate audience with the Successor-Controller, Torv-Varsov.

"I am Skalv-Dalkov, Citizen Successor-Controller," he announced, when led into the simple, austere workroom from which Torv-Varsov controlled the affairs of the planet.

Tov-Varsov put down the report, which he had read before admitting the brain-cell. "Fascinating," he said, "fascinating! You are sure about all of this, I suppose?"

"We made cross-checks from two killer-boats, twelve degrees of the planet's circumference apart, Citizen Successor-Controller," the fish-oil brain-cell said. "There can be no question about it. The signals come from the Horizon Object."

"Which, of course, means that the Horizon Object must be a world like our own, inhabited by intelligent creatures who have attained a high degree of civilization." Tov-Varsov frowned. "You appreciate the implications of this, Citizen Skalv-Dalkov?"

"I have tried not to, Citizen Successor-Controller," the other replied. "I am familiar with the position taken by The Books of Tissé on this issue. This world is the center of the Mind of Vran; the objects in the sky are all trivial, and of small size."

"Yet now we have the direct evidence of instruments far less fallable than the senses," Tov-Varsov replied. "Come now, Citizen, you have been trained as a brain-cell. You should know that, for all He was inspired by Vran, the Blessed Tissé was a scientifically illiterate, semi-skilled body-cell in the anarchic State of his time. Furthermore, his writing, for all that it is the Revealed Word of Vran, was written to be understood by ignorant semi-barbarians."

"But the centricity of this world in the Mind of Vran is a fundamental—" Skalv-Dalkov suddenly remembered just whom he was starting to lecture on theology, and abruptly stopped and closed his mouth, hoping he didn't look as foolish as he felt.

"My son, you are suffering from a lack of faith," Tov-Varsov said, assuming his religious mantle, "coupled with a lack of imagination. Because science has now discovered that the Horizon Object, based upon irrefutable evidence, must be a world like our own, and is probably inhabited with people more or less like ourselves, you feel that the religious doctrine of centricity is somehow threatened. Is that not so?"

Skalv-Dalkov nodded humbly. "That was my

thought, Successor-Controller," he admitted.

"Do you not think that Vran can hold all objects, of whatever size, in his mind?"

"Yes, of course."

"Then size is, clearly, irrelevant in this context. The distinction is clear. Religion is of the spirit, therefore non-physical. Physical measurements, such as size, weight, or distance, are of no relevance. Science is of the body, therefore physical. There can be no possible conflict; each represents truth of a different category."

"I see that now, Successor-Controller."

Tov-Varsov picked up a phone and ordered all his deputies to assemble at once in the conference chamber, and then turned back to Skalv-Dalkov. "This, of course, is a matter to be kept inside the Brain. The body-cells can function only as long as they do not question the doctrines of the Citizen-Originator, or The Books of Tissé. We must suppress any report of this, and amputate any body-cells who may have learned the origin of these signals. We must prepare to gradually change perceptions to coincide with the facts. From now on, there must be no more use of radio in or beyond the Outward Islands."

Chapter Eleven

The radio signals detected on Shining Sister ceased suddenly. For what would have been twenty sleep periods, if anyone had done much sleeping, the giant transmitter beamed its message across space without response. Finally, everyone gave up hope and the effort was halted.

"It's the same thing that happened back in 556," Arlla Hannaro, the head adviser of the Shining Sister Combine, said wearily. "We pick up their signals, and we get very excited over them; we transmit a carefully-designed response back, and then they all stop broadcasting."

They must not know it's coming from us," Karlo Sankangro, the Newspaper Gangs' Combine representative, said. "Although you'd think they'd almost have to. Don't you suppose they have any sort of direction-finders?"

"Yes, I do," Arlla told him. "And I think that's precisely why they go off the air as soon as they pick up our signals. I think they know where the signals are coming from, and I think they're frightened."

"Frightened? In the name of reason, why would

anybody be frightened by a radio message from another planet, a hundred and twenty-five thousand kilo-lances away?'' one of the representatives of a big, independent newspaper gang demanded.

Arlla shrugged. "What do any of us know about their mental processes? All we know is that there are people of some kind there, and they've invented radio recently, so that they are somewhere around our own cultural level. But we know nothing of what they call culture. We don't know what they're interested in, what they think of the universe, what they think of the large object that's always in their sky. We don't even know what they look like. They might have three heads, or be covered with scales like a *pterinnal*, instead of fur. And as far as their not returning our signal—Frasko Kanganno, the head observer at Skystabber, has a theory that Shining Sister may be surrounded by some sort of an electrified atmosphere-layer, as a result of all that water, which would have the effect of increasing the frequency of radio waves passing through it. Which would mean that they can't receive a message sent on the same apparent wave-length as the messages we receive. And if they did receive it, by some fluke, we wouldn't be listening for the response on the wavelength they'd send it."

"What do you think about that?" one of the reporters asked.

"I'm not much impressed with this theory, as a theory, and to tell the truth, neither is Frasko. Don't quote me as saying this, but I think he's merely offering it as an alternative to my own theory because he is emotionally repelled by the idea that Our Sister's Children are afraid to talk to us.

But you can quote me on this—and Frasko, too, he agrees with me: The only way we're going to find out what Shining Sister is really like, and what sort of people our cousins really are, will be to build ourselves a rocket and go there!"

The Shining Sister Combine, at the Storm Valley Rendezvous, was already experimenting in that direction. They had developed a liquid-fuel rocket engine that would burn liquid oxygen and alcohol, and had used it to send a test rocket to an altitude of over fifty thousand lances. One of their scientists had done a workup to demonstrate that a two-stage rocket with that as the first stage could easily put a substantial payload in a low orbit around the planet. A two-stage rocket with that as the second stage could achieve escape velocity with a reasonable payload. By multiplexing the engines, and using a common fuel supply, they could create a massive enough first-stage to be able to lift a manned rocket completely clear of Hetaira, and land a specially designed pod on the surface (or in the water) of Shining Sister.

But nobody could think of a way to carry enough fuel to allow a return flight.

The Balkadranna Gang, at Fall River Rendezvous, inadvertently opened the door to space-travel—among many other things. They were a scientific-research gang, specializing in Physics. Two of their researchers, Voldro and Yanna Balkadranna, had isolated microscopic amounts of the 235-weight isotope of uranium, and established that it could be fissioned, with considerable energy release. They published their findings, and tried to get the necessary mathematical assistance to design a controllable-fission device. It was clear that uncontrolled fission would not be a desirable effect unless one wanted to remove a mountain.

There was a brief flurry of public excitement about this, due to prematurely optimistic statements in the public press. It soon became clear that the harnessing of atomic energy was going to be a long, and expensive, process; it would be a good while before the state of the art would permit of atomic rocket engines. And so interest began to wane in Shining Sister again.

Arlla Hannaro, considering the chemical-fuel rocket problem, decided that it might be feasable to send a manned rocket to Shining Sister which would orbit around it and return and land on her own world. If such a rocket were sent out and returned, with even the poorest high-altitude photographs of the hidden side of the planet, the scientific gain would be enormous, and the public enthusiasm would be incalculably great. With only the slightest urging, the people of Hetaira could develop the sort of mania for Shining Sister that is, in other places, reserved for wars or sporting events. The board of advisers of the Combine decided to allocate funds to make the attempt. There were a series of sedate news-releases, emphasizing the fact that success in this venture would be years coming. Nonetheless the trickle of contributions increased, and kept at a slightly higher level.

The years passed. The Balkadranna Gang, at Fall River Rendezvous, succeeded in separating enough U-235 to build a graphite-moderated reactor which would not only sustain a chain reaction, but would generate enough steam to heat the Rendezvous's buildings and run its power plant. Seeing commercial possibilities in the new power-source, a gang in the Horizon Zone began mining uranite and floated a loan from the Trading Combine to build an extraction and isotope-separation plant.

Arlla Hannaro was killed, in 610, in an explosion at the rocket-engine testing site; her son, Vandro Hannaro, took her place as adviser of advisers. In 614, after an extensive testing program, a multi-step rocket was launched from a firing stand on the north side of Skystabber, aimed to land in the middle of Shining Sister's vast ocean. It was radar tracked as it lofted out of the atmosphere, circled the planet twice, and then headed across the void separating the sister worlds. Unfortunately, a component failure caused the small rocket motor in the last stage to fire its mid-course correction at the wrong time, and to expend its fuel entirely in that one shot. The radar-trackers then had the pleasure of watching the spacecraft miss Shining Sister and pass out of contact, going in the direction of the Star-Cluster.

The contributions to support the work of the Combine dwindled off after that. Most of the loose money was being invested in nuclear-power projects. Vandro Hannaro and his associates were not particularly displeased about this last; they had long felt that the development of nuclear power and the necessary improvement in nuclear technology that it would foster would be of great utility in the eventual conquest of space. Less pleasant was the outburst of uranium wars, reminiscent of the oil-wars of the previous century.

Finally a three-stage, unmanned rocket was launched that successfully dumped the final stage into the great ocean of Shining Sister's near side. Two years later the rocket that was to circle Shining Sister and photograph the hidden side was built; it left the treasury of the Combine empty, and a staggering total of unpaid debts hanging over the advisers' heads. The excitement that was generated by the project, however, was tremendous; it was impossible to hear anything else talked of.

"A lot of public interest, yes," Vandro said, rubbing the fur of his head nervously, as though he had fleas. "But everybody thinks the job is just about done, now, and there's no need for further contributions. If we had some way of raising a little more money—"

"A *lot* more money," his chief assistant said.

"Look, Vandro," an old man who had been one of Arlla's assistants, and who might, for all either of them knew, have been Vandro's father, said. "The rocket is designed to carry three: pilot, instrumenter, and relief. Well, the first two have to be well trained professionals, so they will be able to react correctly in case anything, no matter how unlikely, goes wrong. But couldn't you send a relief up with just perfunctory training—say, half a year —if you had to?"

"We could, I suppose," Vandro agreed, "but what would be the point?"

"Look, suppose we sell the third place on the rocket. There must be thousands of people who'd pay well for a chance to go on that trip!"

"No individual could pay well enough," Vandro

said, "not even if his gang financed him. It would only be a drop in the bucket. Have you any idea—" He paused, a strange look on his face.

"What is it, Vandro?" his assistant demanded.

"I have an idea."

"Thank goodness. From the way you looked, I thought you had an attack of stomach-pain."

"No, seriously, I have what might be quite an idea," Vandro said. He turned to the old man. "And it's *your* idea, Zalgo."

"My idea?"

"That's right. *Chance,* you said. Well, that's it! *Chance!* We'll have a lottery!"

Vandro was right. The idea caught the popular imagination. It was understood, of course, that the winner would be required to meet certain physical and mental standards; but it was also realized that if the individual failed, he or she would have no trouble selling the winning ticket for many times its original cost. Gangs of speculators bought blocks of tickets, intending to do just that. Vandro began to worry, as the money poured in, that there was something he hadn't thought of, something that was going to go wrong, causing the whole idea to blow up in their—his—face. He could, for example, imagine the outburst of murderous fury which would rock the planet at the slightest suspicion of fraud. He had a recurrent dream, in which the numbering machine on the press had jammed, turning out thousands of tickets with the same number, which then happened to win.

The drawing was held at the headquarters of the Trading Combine, at Timber Lake, with the entire board of advisers watching over it. The winning number was flashed by telephone and radio around the world, which then held its collective breath to see who held the ticket.

It was three sleep-periods before the winner, a girl named Lylla Rovodorro, called in to claim her prize. A member of a small ranching gang on the plains, Lylla had been up-country at the time of the drawing, and had taken three sleep-periods to get back to somewhere with a telephone. Her arrival at Storm Valley Rendezvous, two sleep-periods later, was televised and relayed everywhere.

It was almost three years before the rocket was ready, during which time Lylla became a proficient pilot. A huge crowd, some coming all the way from the Outer Hemisphere, began gathering near the firing-point a few sleep-periods before the launch time. The rocket was hauled up onto the launching-track; the crew entered, closing the air-lock behind them, and strapped in. They did a quick pre-flight check, and signalled ready. In the firing bunker, Vandro closed the switch. The roar of the rockets could be heard for five thousand lances in all directions. Slowly at first, and then with ever-increasing speed, the rocket made its run along the launch-track, and then majestically rose into the atmosphere, and away.

Tov-Varsov was no longer Successor-Controller. Krav-Torov, the Controller of Spiritual and Political Orthodoxy, had eliminated him in a lightning coup twelve years before, along with his designated successor, Lev-Lonov. The body-cells and lower brain-cells were satisfied with the official explanation that Lev-Lonov had murdered the Citizen Successor-Controller, and then had been am-

putated by the patriotic and loyal Krav-Torov,
who had saved the Organic State from criminal
usurpation. It was noted that Krav-Torov never
appointed a successor to his own previous position,
but kept the machinery of the temporal and spiritual secret police tightly in his own hand.

Like everybody else on the upper policy level, he
had been thoroughly familiarized with the case of
the mysterious radio signals believed to originate
from the Horizon Object, and with the possible
dangers of allowing radio to be used on the Outward Islands. However, radio was too useful a
tool, both for communication and for the continuous propaganda with which the brain-cells bar-
raged the body-cells, to just give it up. On the continents safely shadowed from the neighboring
planet, the broadcasting and relay stations multiplied. Every Temple of Tissé reared its antenna-
spire; every village and town and agricultural center had its tower. Every citizen had a cheap, fixed-
frequency receiver. The Creed of Puzzá and the
doctrines of Dov-Soglov, and the will of Successor-
Controller Krav-Torov, were reiterated incessant-
ly.

On the twelfth anniversary of the Martyrdom of
Tov-Varsov and the frustration of the Treason of
Lev-Lonov, every radio was turned on, all the
variable-frequency radios of the higher brain-cells
were tuned to the same wavelength. Priests intoned
thanks to Vran for the deliverance of the True
Faith and the scientifically organized State. An official historian read the carefully edited account of
the courage and patriotism of the Citizen
Successor-Controller.

Then, in the midst of the festivities, a strange

signal intruded: a bar of music, a voice in an alien
tongue, and a second bar of music. The reaction
was clear and swift, but due to the complications of
the day, it was some time before the rebroadcast
stations could be ordered off the air. Even then, it
was found that the mysterious signal, repeated over
and over, and occasionally varied by what sounded
like more unintelligible language, was being received by public radio in one sector after another
across the face of the planet.

The detection stations, maintained against possible subversive use of the radio, quickly swung
into action. At first their readings did not appear to
make any sense; but the technicians quickly figured
out how to interpret them. What they were listening to was a signal being broadcast from a moving
body, travelling considerably faster than the speed
of sound, and about a thousand leagues straight
up. Its path, they soon established, was a great
loop inward from the Horizon Zone, around the
planet, and then back out again.

Orv-Gorov, the Dean of Archpriests, met with
Karv-Torov and the top deputies of the State on
the upper terrace of the huge building which had
been constructed by Rav-Razkov around the Shop
of the Cobbler. The Citizen Successor-Controller
drummed on the table-top with his long middle fingers.

"You all heard this thing," he said, "either directly or in recordings. It would seem to be identi-
cal with the signals heard in the time of the late
Citizen Tov-Varsov, and, for that matter, those received during the war against the Zaithuan here-
tics."

"It would seem so," Yorrov-Voppov, the Deputy for Technological Conformity said.

"And what are we to conclude from this?" Karv-Torov asked, using a formula from the Questions of Faith section in The Books of Tissé.

"Well, Citizen," Yorrov-Voppov said, "the present signals are clearly coming from an upper-atmosphere vehicle which is circumnavigating the planet. The question is, undoubtedly, where did this vehicle come from?

"As I see it, there are only two possibilities; either it came from somewhere on this planet, or it came from somewhere out there." He gestured in a vaguely upward direction.

"Continue," Karv-Torov said, not visibly impressed by the analysis so far.

"If it came from somewhere on this planet, then we have to assume that there are secret laboratories and workshops of some group unknown to us, and that they have a higher level of technology than we, ourselves. This presents two questions to which there are no rational answers: first, if this group exists, why does it choose now to reveal itself, and why by this means; and second, if it is as superior technologically as one would have to assume from this ship circling the planet, why bother hiding itself at all? Unless someone can come up with an answer to these two questions, then I think we must assume the vehicle, and thus the transmissions, to be extra-planet in origin. This hypothesis is supported by the evidence of the earlier transmissions, which seemed to originate on the Horizon Object. This would seem to establish beyond conjecture that the Horizon Object is a planet like our own, and is inhabited by some form of intelligent life."

"But it's all absurd!" the Dean of Archpriests declared. "There are clear statements in The Books as to what the heavens are like, and nowhere is there mentioned other planets like onto this one. And then to assume that, not only is the Horizon Object a planet with living beings on it, but that these beings can build a vehicle which can carry them across hundreds of thousands of leagues of empty space, something which, as I understand, we ourselves cannot do—"

"Citizen-Priest Orv-Gorov, it is you who speak absurdities," Krav-Torov rebuked. "We have the evidence of observations based on the best scientific instruments. You, on the other hand, are calling something absurd merely because *you* do not wish to believe in it. It goes against something you read in a book. One of The Books, perhaps, but still only a book. On the other hand, balanced against your book, is the presence of a very real object circling our planet, sending radio-signals to everything it passes over. Music! No, Citizen-Priest; despite The Books, the Horizon Object is a world like our own. And its people would seem to have been trying to communicate with us for years, and they now have built a machine enabling them to cross space and drop in.

"This is the situation which confronts us, whatever The Books say. Now let us consider realistically what we are going to do about it."

"We must consider the effect on the body-cells," one of the deputies said. "This thing is going to destroy their faith in The Books, which is fundamental to everything else."

"Not necessarily," Krav-Torov said. "Not if it's handled right. After all, the body-cells are not encouraged to read The Books of Tissé for themselves, even those few who can read by themselves. We must now begin to prepare them. Discover, for the greater glory of Vran, that there is a possibility that the Horizon Object is a world like our own, and that those signals that everybody is talking about must have come from there. The Citizen-Priest can find an appropriate chapter in The Books of Tissé that predicts that such a discovery will be made at this time. Can't you, Priest?"

Orv-Gorov bent his head. "Unfathomable are the ways of Vran," he said.

"There's a great mission and a great opportunity for you, Dean of Archpriests," Krav-Torov said. "Consider: the inhabitants of other worlds, now that we admit to the existence of other worlds, may well be ignorant of the sacred truths of The Books of Tissé, and all else concerning Vran. It will be our duty to instruct them. You must start preparing brain-cells for this function."

"That is so," Orv-Gorov said, thoughtfully.

"And we must make plans to acquaint them with the advantages of the scientific structure of the Organic State."

"I wonder if these people—things—whatever they are—in the circling vessel have landed anywhere," Tav-Frakov, the Deputy Controller of Food Production said. "Perhaps, if they have, we could find them and amputate them. Then we could take their ship for study, and get rid of all other signs of their presence, and pass the whole thing off as a miracle. Within a few years the event will be forgotten."

Several of the others murmured agreement. Krav-Torov grimaced and slammed both hands down on the table-top. "Great Vran, pity me, who am advised by imbeciles!" he cried. "Do you think those who circle our world are the only inhabitants of their world, or that their vehicle of space is unique?"

"No, Citizen Successor-Controller. That is why I advised amputating those who may have landed here."

"Yes? And have you thought beyond your nose? Have you considered what would happen then? Has it occurred to you that those who sent this space-vehicle will miss it when it fails to return? That they will send further vehicles to find out what happened? That if they discover that their representatives have been amputated, they might not be pleased?" He glared at all those around him. "Have we the technology to build such a machine? No! Therefore it is clear that the residents of the Horizon Object are scientifically and technically in advance of us. What sort of weapons do you suppose such people would have, knives and clubs?"

"But then, if they are our technological superiors, they may conquer us if we allow them a foothold here."

Krav-Torov shook his head. "If they don't hear from this expedition, then they'll only send a bigger expedition—one big enough to land in force and start operations against us. But if we receive the first party in friendship, we may postpone hostilities at least long enough to learn just what we have to deal with. If we're careful and clever, we can keep them off guard. They will be able to tell, without much dispute, that they are our technological superiors. This may lull them into thinking that they are also our superiors in other ways. They will not feel threatened, and will remain friendly. It will be to their advantage to be friendly at first. Although our technological superiors, they will be vastly outnumbered."

"That is so," someone agreed.

"We will, therefore, keep them friendly as long as possible, and at least long enough to learn their science before a war starts. And, Citizens, I have enough faith in the holy religion of Tissé and the Organic State to believe that, given time, we will outstrip them. Then we shall see whose planet is conquered by whom!"

Vandro Hannaro, waiting at Storm Valley Rendezvous, watched the disc of Shining Sister grow in his television screen, as the camera in the nose of the rocket sped toward it. The voices of Dantro Fanzagarro, the pilot, and Karnna Lassantro, the instrumenter, and Lylla Rovorrido, came through, describing the effects of the acceleration they had endured—much less serious than had been predicted—and laughing about their misadventures in the unfamiliar weightlessness.

Time passed. The watchers worked in shifts, staring at the screen and discussing the problems that came up with the crew. The Horizon Islands grew larger and plainer, and many of the smaller islands of the Central Sea became visible. Then the spacecraft skipped by the rim of the planet, and passed it, and the gravity of Shining Sister checked it in its arrow-straight path, reached out and pulled it into a parabolic orbit. For the first time the watchers saw the seven continents of Shining Sister surrounding the Central Sea, and the great, shallow expanse of ocean that was the invisible side.

"We have picked up radio signals from below," Karnna reported. "I don't know what it means, but every radio transmitter on the planet is sending the same thing—voices speaking, and what sounds like chanting in regular poetic meter."

"Maybe they have picked you up on radar, if they have radar, and are welcoming you," Vandro suggested.

"That could be. At any rate, we have started broadcasting our friendship message on the same wave-length; so they'll certainly pick it up. We're going to be passing behind the planet in a few seconds, so it will be a while before you hear from us again. Think good thoughts."

"All right. We'll be waiting to hear from you when you come around. Be careful with your fuel; don't get carried away and try to go too low. You'll need it for maneuvering your way back here."

The screen went gray, and a second later the carrier wave of the radio vanished. Vandro rose stiffly and went to a couch. The others turned from the screens, some to lie down, some for food and tea, and some of the less weary just to sit around and talk.

Somebody shook Vandro awake when the screens came to life again, with a beautiful view of their own planet as seen around the crescent arm of Shining Sister. A short time later Dantro

Fanzagarro's voice came over the speakers.

"Vandro, your mother was right; they are afraid of us. I don't know what all the chanting and yelling was about, but it certainly wasn't to welcome us. Almost as soon as we began sending on their wavelength, everything stopped. We haven't been able to raise anything since."

"Maybe they are keeping radio silence to better receive you."

"I don't believe it. We varied the recorded message with our own voices. We sent them number-series signals. We tapped things out with a buzzer. We tried everything. It just wasn't any use. As soon as we began sending, their stations all went off the air. We did get some great pictures of the surface with the telephoto cameras. We saw cities, towns, ships, even a few aircraft flying below us. The aircraft seemed fairly primitive, to my eyes."

The return trip took six sleep-periods. The watchers at Storm Valley and on Skystabber, and at thousands of stations around the Outer Hemisphere slept only in fitful snatches, and not at all when the rocket entered its series of braking elipses. The whole planet held its breath until the ram-jet engines on the wingtips gulped in enough air and flamed into life. And when it bellied down for a perfect landing along the ten-kilolance runway prepared in the middle of the Burning Desert, telephone bells jangled in the editorial offices of a thousand newspaper gangs, whistles and bells and cannon proclaimed that the first voyagers to Shining Sister had returned safely.

The photographs taken on the spiral sweep over

the Outer Hemisphere were carefully developed, enlarged, and examined. They were able to confirm Dantro's opinion that he had seen cities and towns down below. Under high resolution, they were even able to make out individual houses, squares, some roads and other artifacts. It was clearly a densely-populated, and apparently a highly-civilized world. Imagination supplied innumerable details; arguments grew heated. Maps were made. And all Hetaira resolved as one that someday, as soon as possible, a landing must be made.

The Alvararro Gang had already developed a nuclear-power rocket engine which could be used as an out-of-atmosphere auxilliary drive for space ships. Because its exhaust was poisonously radioactive, it could not be used to supply power for takeoffs and landings. After considering many possibilities, it was decided to build a large nuclear-powered ship to go into orbit around Shining Sister, and chemical shuttle-rockets for planetary landings. The amount of fuel necessary to rise to a low orbit and intersect a waiting mother-ship was much less than the amount needed for a high orbit, or for free flight in space.

The work took years. A whole technology had to be created to build a large object in space. The shuttle-rockets themselves were perfected during this period, by the simple expedient of building them at a rate sufficient to put one into orbit about every ten sleep-periods. The rockets lifted structural materials and supplies and oxygen and fuel and water and food and workers. And slowly, with many a change in detail as new things were learned along the way, the spaceship grew in low orbit around the planet.

When finished, the ship was a huge globe, which could carry a crew of fifty; it could stay in space, fully manned, for a number of years. She carried six long shuttle-rockets, each twice the size of the one which had made the circuit around Shining Sister ten years before. Her captain was the man who had given the project his single-minded devotion from his mother's breast, Vandro Hannaro.

Chapter Twelve

Two hundred hours after she had blasted out of her orbit around the home planet, the *Sister's Visitor* was in orbit above her destination. This time there was no attempt at contact by radio. Shuttle Rocket Number One was launched even as the ship's orbit was being stabilized. It spiralled over the Outer Hemisphere inside the atmosphere, using ramjet power to pull it quite close to the surface several times, and rocket-assisted jet to take it back out again. By the time *Sister's Visitor* began its second orbit, two planetary diameters from the surface, the shuttle rocket was locked back in its pad, and the film from its specially-designed cameras was already on the drying-racks.

As the photographs were studied and analyzed, the space ship slowly spiralled closer to the planet, to take up an orbit a mere one-third of a planetary diameter off. A primary landing site was picked for the delta-winged shuttle craft, and four of them dropped free of the ship and jetted in toward the planet.

Vandro Hannaro piloted the lead shuttle; his copilot was Lylla Rovorrido, the girl who had won a place on the first expedition ten years before. With them were a physicist from the Balkadranna Gang, named Yssa, and Zandro Garvanno, the biologist. The two shuttle-craft that followed him down were piloted by Dantro Fanzagarro and Karnna Lassantro, the other members of the first expedition; they carried only pilot and copilot, and were loaded with enough fuel to enable at least one of the three to return to the mother ship. The fourth shuttle-craft, instead of landing with the other three, used its ramjet engines to explore the planet from the upper atmosphere.

They had selected the long, narrow continent, which, as they would learn, was named Dudak; and they had picked an area of what looked like open farmland, cross-gridded with roads, some thirty kilolances south of a large town. There were, Vandro saw, a small clump of buildings with flat roofs, and several tall smokestacks. It could be the village of a sugar-planting gang. He glanced back and forth between the map made from the aerial photographs to the screen connected with the pick-ups on the wing-tips, which gave a binocular view of the ground ahead, clear of the retro fire jet flames.

If it was a sugar plantation, they got their sugar from something entirely different from the tubers grown on his own world; the crop seemed to be high stuff, for there was a distinct shadow-line between the standing and harvested areas. There was a section already harvested, big enough to set down all three rockets, using the short-field stall-and-drop landing techniques that had been worked out and practiced time after time over the past three years. It was about five hundred lances from the clump of flat-roofed buildings.

They were down to two hundred lances, now, with the ramjet engines firing at full thrust. Below, they had been seen. There were vehicles on the roads, and small dots that must be people in the fields; and all were hurrying frantically away from where the shuttle craft were going to come down. As they dropped a bit further, Vandro could see that the people were reassuringly humanoid—erect bipeds, with two visible arms.

"Take control, Lylla. Put her down so that our triangle apex will point toward that village. Over about there," he indicated on the screen. "That should give you enough room."

Lylla glanced critically at the indicated area. "With a whole lance to spare, I'd say," she said.

"I have confidence in you," Vandro told her. He picked up the hand-phone and called the two shuttles behind him. "Follow us in. Maintain the fifty-lance triangle. Kwalvo, do you hear me? Where are you?"

The pilot of the shuttle that wasn't landing called in, "Kwalvo to Vandro. I hear you easily. I am about three hundred kilolances away now, doing a photo run over what looks like a small industrial city. I'll be over your landing-site in about ten minutes, when you need me for the fireworks."

"Good. Stay about four thousand lances up, when you come in. Be ready to drop lower if the natives prove too hostile for the display, as planned. If it turns out that we need a bombing run, I'll want extreme precision."

"You'll get it," Kwalvo promised.

Yssa Balkadranna flipped the switch on the big screen in front of them to show the feed from the rotating scanner in the nose of the shuttle. "Take a look, Vandro," she called, "There's some kind of aircraft headed toward us from the direction of the village. I'm not sure, but I think it just took off from there. Can't tell yet whether it intends to be hostile."

"Okay, Yssa. Lylla, put us down." He studied the image on the screen. The plane was a big thing, a low-wing monoplane with twin jets on pods above each wing. It looked like a transport.

Lylla brought the shuttle down, cutting the jets. It bumped along the field for a few seconds, as the great flaps extended and killed the remaining speed. The other shuttles came in right behind it, taking their places on the ground in an equilateral triangle.

Vandro unstrapped himself from his seat, taking his pistol belt and putting it on. The others were freeing themselves; Yssa slung a belt of hand-grenades, and Zandro checked the clip on an auto-carbine and then slung it over his shoulder.

At the last second, Vandro picked up the micro-phone. "Okay, we're going out," he said. "Now, excuse me for repeating this, but I'd rather be neu-rotically redundant than miss something. We sim-ply can't have this first contact with Our Sister's Children ruined by bloodshed. So I must go beyond 'don't start anything' to 'don't use your weapons unless it looks like they're going to massacre us,' and then, let me add, shoot to disable rather than kill."

The native aircraft, a broad-winged, coppery-gleaming contraption, was circling over them at about a hundred and fifty lances. As Vandro watched it on his screen, it opened a pair of doors in its belly; a maneuver that reminded him of the explosive-dropping aircraft of the Rim Country oil wars of the Fifth Century. He wondered what sort of explosives these people used, and how badly it could damage the titanium skin of the shuttle-craft. If it damaged the exterior heat-shield, it would not prevent the shuttles from taking off and rejoining the mother ship in orbit, so that wasn't an immediate worry. Although the carbon-filament skin would have to be repaired before they could come back down again.

"Dantro, Karnna; cancel that instruction to exit now. Keep your airlocks closed," he yelled into the microphone. "Kwalvo! Hurry on over here. I think we need your demonstration of moral superiority about now. There's a plane buzzing us that needs impressing."

"Kwalvo to Vandro; on our way. Watch for us at about two hundred lances over that airplane."

Rylla was operating the lateral pickup manually, and now she rotated it to keep the circling airplane centered. It seemed undecided as to what to do. Either waiting for some first move by them, Vandro thought, or waiting for some word from a distant decision-maker. Vandro switched on the exterior microphones, and from them came two distinct noises; the sound of the big four-jet aircraft overhead, and a high, intermittent screaming that might be some sort of alarm siren from the village.

Then, suddenly, came a third sound that drowned out everything else—a deafening, ear-battering roar, like a great waterfall, a huge blast-furnace, and a continuous thunderstorm combined. A wide ribbon of red smoke appeared in the cloud-fleeced blue sky, curving in a full circle around the three grounded shuttlecraft. The copper-glistening aircraft banked to the left, turned quickly, and shot away out of the circle.

"Smart boy," Vandro commented. "He's never seen anything like that before, and has no idea of what it is. And, whatever it turns out to be, he doesn't want any part of it. All right, let's open her up and go outside."

They rotated the airlock open and extended the elevator. The other two shuttle-craft were also unbuttoning; they could see Dantro and Karnna and their co-pilots, also armed and laden with equipment, come dropping down the seven-lance descent to the ground. "That ought to impress any native who's watching," Vandro said, climbing sedately into the elevator. "It impresses me."

High overhead, Kwalvo Yarragarro was making another circle, a hundred lances higher, and five hundred wider; but this time without the noise. When he had finished that, he changed his smoke from red to blue and slashed a straight line across, and then bisected it directly overhead with another. From the mother ship, far off in orbit, it would be visible telescopically as two smears of red with a smear of blue sandwiched between. But to an observer directly at zenith, it would be a pair of red circles center-crossed in blue. That was the impression Vandro wanted to create—that the observer, with a whole space-fleet, was directly overhead.

The earth had been blackened and burned in patches around the three landing-craft, where the down-thrusting ramjets had scorched a landing-path. The ground under the ships was littered with bits of vegetable-matter and covered with the stubble of the thick, pulpy plants that had recently been harvested from it. Some patches were still burning. Vandro and those with him stomped over to these patches, breathing thanks for their ankle-high boots and leather trousers. They used portable fire extinguishers on the burning places, and then stamped and kicked out any places that looked like they might be still smouldering. Then the crews of the three ships met at the center of the triangle and set down their cases of equipment.

There was a piece of native farm machinery sitting just about in the center—a wheeled thing with a big fork, which looked as though it had been used to gather and bundle whatever the crop was. Vandro made up a few inventive new cursewords, when he suddenly realized that he had completely missed seeing the gadget from the air, and they must have missed it by no more than a couple of arm-widths.

A strip a hundred lances wide had already been cut through the field, extending from a distant clump of tall, tree-like fauna, past the ships, to the clump of buildings and smokestacks some three hundred lances in front of them. On either side, the crops were still standing. The plant looked like giant club-mosses, stalks two lances high and thick as a man's leg at the knee. Karnna picked up a half-burned bit of plant-detritus from the ground and sniffed at it. "Doesn't smell as though it had a very high sugar content," she said. "Obviously carbon-oxygen-hydrogen, though. They might use the stuff for roughage for whatever kinds of herbivorous animals they raise, or—"

"Here they come!" Yssa said, pointing across the fields, then raising her binoculars.

There were four large trucks with boxy bodies, that looked like they were probably armed and armored, and ahead of them came two small open cars, each carrying half a dozen humanoid figures. One of the cars came on toward the grounded shuttle-craft, the other, and the trucks, began circling slowly around, at about two hundred lances. They didn't make any attempt to preserve any of the crop, but just plowed it under their wide wheels as they went.

Yssa had her glasses trained on the approaching open car. "Oh! They're horrible!" she cried. "They have no fur; just some hideous stuff like grass on their heads. And they're covered with clothing, all over, from what I can tell. The little bits of skin that are sticking out are green-gray, like a swamp-eel's."

"Restrain yourself, Yssa," Karnna said. "Remember, we probably look just as hideous to them."

"Ridiculous, Karnna," Yssa said. "Why, just look at them, and then look at us. Any unbiased person would have to admit that we're rather handsome people, and they're monsters."

The open car came to a stop just outside the triangle of the landing-craft. Four of the six occupants got out and stood talking for a moment. The driver remained in his seat, as did the one who sat beside him (her? Yssa wondered; she couldn't tell —all the ones she could see seemed to be of the same sex. They looked male, but she'd like to have seen a female for comparison), who was crouched behind something that looked like a heavy, rapid-fire gun.

The four who descended took off their belts and put them on the seats of the vehicle, and then advanced toward the Hetairans, their arms extended in front of them. Vandro nodded to himself, pleased. To lay aside weapons and approach with plainly empty hands seemed like an obvious peace-gesture to him; the fact that these natives thought so too was a sign that their mental processes were not totally unsimilar.

They had six fingers, the two outside ones thumbs, he noted, and made a small bet with himself that their mathematics would be based on a duodecimal system. Their faces were broad, with wide mouths and heavy jaws, bulging eyes and erect, pointed ears; but all the parts seemed to be in the right places. The most alien-looking thing about them was their body baldness—assuming it carried through under their clothing—and the strange stuff on their heads, which was definitely not fur. Yssa was right, despite—or, perhaps, because of—the great similarities in what one might call gross appearance, they did look pretty horrible.

The circling shuttle-craft came roaring down for one more pass, with the sound-maker on again, and the newcomers ducked their heads as one, although the puff of red smoke it released was a good five hundred lances over their heads. Dantro Fanzagarro, kneeling beside the radio transmitter, began reporting into it, and Lylla kept the television camera aimed at the delegation of Shining Sister's unpleasant-looking children.

Chapter Thirteen

It was three sleep-periods later when the Successor-Controller and his entourage arrived at the Doroda Alcohol Center on Dudak. Before going out to look at the great ships that had landed in the *narga*-field, they paused to refresh themselves after the journey—Krav-Torov didn't want to look tired or worn when meeting the aliens; probably the most important confrontation he'd have during his whole ministry.

His car headed the small convoy that left the distillery buildings and headed for the field of *narga*-stubble. "Slower, Citizen Driver," he instructed as they entered the field, "and a little to the left; when we get closer, half-circle around them to give me a look at them."

"Obedience, Citizen Controller-Successor."

The car slowed, and Krav-Torov leaned across Harv-Sarov, on his right. The three space vehicles were ahead; great streamlined shapes in black and silver, larger than any aircraft ever built by the Organic State, at least three times as large as anything currently flying. They had huge jet engine pods on their triangular wings, with great air-intake scoops that looked as though they closed up for streamlining when they weren't in use. A cluster of rocket nozzles came out of the rear of the strange craft.

Much as their size impressed him, it didn't seem that they were large enough to carry sufficient fuel for the return trip. They could have had disposable tanks for the trip across, but if so they were obviously disposed of already. Scientists working on the problem for him had hypothesized that the reason why the earlier ship had not landed was that it could not have carried enough fuel to lift itself out of the gravity well and crossed space to its home planet again.

But a ship could carry enough fuel to reach a low orbit and return to the ground several times. Which meant that these ships had probably been launched from some gigantic space-travelling vehicle, which must even now be orbiting around his planet. If these, then, were indeed mere landing-craft, the thought of what the ship that carried them must be like awed him, as did the scientific and organizational abilities of its builders. These beings must certainly have some sort of an Organic State, probably one more highly developed than his own.

He had been worrying about the inadequacy of the troops available, and wishing that the Organic State, after the bloody extinction of its last rival, had not allowed its armed forces to deteriorate. But now he realized that no army that had ever been fielded on his planet, not even the forces which had marched to the conquest of Dudak in 2078, would have been of any use to him against the beings who had built these ships. The only hope

for the survival of the Organic State lay in conciliation and avoidance of conflict—at least until the
science of these aliens could be appropriated and
applied.

The cars stopped at the edge of the triangle
bounded by the three shuttle-craft, and everybody,
even the drivers, got out and stared at the group
around the tables that had been set up at the center. Krav-Torov spared a hasty glance at Skrov-
Rogov, the supervisor of the Doroda Alcohol Center, and his assistants, and then turned his full attention to examining the aliens.

He had expected to find beings different from
himself, but he was shocked at the extent of the
difference. These creatures were at least a head
taller than any of his own race, and red in color.
They wore leather trousers and vests, and short
boots, and carried what looked like weapons at
their belts. One of his race dressed that way would
have looked scantily-clad, but these beings didn't.
It was, perhaps, because of the body-covering of
some kind of fine down which extended to every
visible part of their anatomy. No, not down, he
corrected himself as he approached the tables; it
was finer, as fine as the nap of velvet. The color
was not uniform. One of them had a pinkish splash
across its flat-nosed, triangular-eared face; another, scarlet elsewhere, was almost white under its
chin.

They were, he was suddenly startled to notice,
missing a thumb on each hand. It would have been
the under-thumb when the two hands were extended and clasping each other. He also noted dif-
ferences between the aliens in physical structure,

which were almost certainly secondary sexual characteristics. Like his own race, these aliens would seem to be gamogenetically-reproducing mammals. That was reassuring; it promised a common psychological base. Although, he reminded himself, the ability to understand another's psychology did not necessarily equate with the ability to get along. The *svarps* were gamogenetically-reproduced mammals, of whom there was a folk-saying, "As dirty and disgusting as a *svarp.*"

This party seemed to consist of four males and four females. He wondered, idly, which was the dominant sex.

The aliens had set up quite a bit of apparatus around the field, and Krav-Torov examined it as best he could as he strode toward the central tables. There was what looked like a portable radio. One of the males was beside it, talking into the handphone. A large, angular, plastic or painted-metal box with a wide lens in its face sat on a heavy tripod. A female was keeping it pointed toward him and his party. Some sort of camera, he supposed, and then realized with a start that, for all he knew, it could be a deadly weapon. There were a few more metal or plastic boxes, studded with dials, levers, and knobs; two of them had large screens which glowed with bluish light and on which pictures shifted.

The tops of the two tables were littered with pads of paper and books, and what looked like oversized photograph-folios. To the left of the tables was a big, white plastic board, on its own stand something like an artist's easel. There were drawings on it; diagrams of some sort done in colored grease-pencil. One of Skrov-Rogov's subordinates and one of the alien females seemed to have been using it to explain something to each other.

When Citizen Successor-Controller Krav-Torov reached the tables in the middle of the triangle, Supervisor Skrov-Rogov and the rest of his party rose from their seats, and the one who had been trying to converse with the alien female put down his grease-pencil. They all gave him the Organicist salute and bowed deeply, holding the bow for perhaps an exaggerated length of time, following Skrov-Rogov's lead, to show the aliens the importance of their visitor. The aliens stared at this happening, and then spoke to each other in queer, high-pitched voices. No doubt, Krav-Torov thought, they were trying to decide just how important he was among his own kind.

"Tell them, Skrov-Rogov," he said, "tell them who I am."

Skrov-Rogov turned to the alien male he had been talking to. "Name Krav-Torov," he said, indicating the Successor-Controller. "Big high man for all people this world."

The alien advanced toward Krav-Torov, grimacing in what was probably his version of a friendly smile. Krav-Torov resisted the urge to take a step backward with each step the alien took forward.

"Name Vandro Hannaro," the alien said, slowly and carefully, and only slightly squeaky. "People my world friends people your world. Your world, my world, sisters; your people, my people, sisters' children."

Krav-Torov looked at Skrov-Rogov with respectful surprise. To have taught these aliens so much of the language in the few days since their arrival had been a considerable feat. He made a mental note to have Citizen Skrov-Rogov's brain-cell category revised upward very sharply.

He tapped himself on the chest. "Name Krav-Torov. My world glad people your world come," he said. "Your world, my world, good friends always. Learn much from each other. Welcome."

"We learn much, your world. We want know all, your world. We work much time, come your world," the alien said. He gestured toward the screens with the glowing pictures. "Learn much, much to learn."

Krav-Torov turned toward the screens and stepped closer, so he could make out the pictures. One was a view of the country around Doroda Alcohol Center, as seen from about three kilometers overhead; the point-of-view was shifting slowly, circling around the complex. The other screen showed a magnification of the scene in the first. In it he could see the three great shuttle-craft, and the grouped tables and chairs, and the equipment, and the people and aliens inside the triangle. He could even make himself out, staring at the screen. Then the scene in the magnified image drifted, and the cars in which he had arrived came into view on one side, to move off the other, followed by the armored trucks, the stand of unharvested *nerga*-plants, and then the massed infantry and combat-vehicles and artillery deployed a league and a half away, waiting on his word. All of this, in plain sight on this strange screen!"

"Citizen Skrov-Rogov," he said, working to keep his voice calm, casual. "What sort of devices are those screens?"

"It seems to be a thing like radio, Citizen Successor-Controller," Skrov-Rogov answered, "except that it transmits pictures instead of sound. We don't know enough of each other's languages yet for them to explain it in any technical way, but that's the basic idea. That box over there, with the lens set into the front, is picking up what's happening here and sending the pictures, in continuous motion, to another spacecraft circling overhead. And that one, in turn, is sending views of the, ah, countryside."

Wonderful! Krav-Torov thought. If we make one hostile move, every alien on the planet not only knows about it, but sees pictures of it. Then the bombs begin to fall. He wondered what sort of bombs they'd be—explosive, fire, poison gas, strange disintegrating rays, little puffs of smoke that turn us into vegetables? Vran only knew which of the endless possibilities.

Krav-Torov took a deep breath. "You have done well, Citizen Skrov-Rogov," he said. "You will turn the management of your farms and distillery over to your immediate subordinate. I'm ordering you immediately re-classified to Category Four. From now on, you'll maintain contact with these beings, and coordinate the work of exchanging linguistic and other information with them. You will follow such directives as you are from time to time given, always keeping in mind that your prime directive is to gain and hold the friendship of these beings at any cost. Have you got that?"

"Yes, Citizen Successor-Controller."

"Remember," Krav-Torov said, stepping close to Skrov-Rogov and dropping his voice to a whisper. "Gain their trust. Make friends with them. Learn their language. Learn their technology. Call on what expert help you need. The resources of the State are yours. Steady increasing success will be rewarded."

"Yes, Citizen Successor-Controller."

"There is a corollary that I don't think we need discuss," Krav-Torov continued. "And that is the price of failure."

"I understand, Citizen Successor-Controller."

Mysterious and deep is the Mind of Vran! Strange and secret are the thoughts of Vran! Incomprehensible are the ways of Vran! Skrov-Rogov repeated this litany to himself piously. How had the Hand of Vran worked to single him out this way! His transfer to Doroda Alcohol Center had actually been a demotion. He had held a much better position at Urava, in the central office of the Bureau of Agrarian Industry Control, until a superior had made an outrageous blunder and had needed a scapegoat. At the time Skrov-Rogov had thought himself lucky not to have been amputated; it never occurred to him to harbor any bitterness about what was plainly a legitimate act of bureaucratic self-defense. He would have done the same, had their positions been reversed.

Now, having tried his loyalty to the machinery of the State, behold how Vran had rewarded him! That he should be given the credit for the fact that these aliens had developed a superb system for teaching and learning languages seemed every bit as just as that he should bear the blame for his superior's idiocy.

Skrov-Rogov soon found himself as the Deputy-Controller in charge of the Agency for Communications With and Technological Studies Of the Visitors from the Horizon Object. It was set up as a regular Control Bureau in miniature. Using the authority given him by the Citizen Successor-Controller, he took over what had been the country estate of one of the wealthy landowners of the old Dudakan Confederacy, now a rest-resort for upper-category brain-cells, and converted it into lodgings for the aliens and headquarters for himself and his assistants. A landing-field for the aliens' shuttlecraft was provided, and the entire company of the orbiting mother-ship, at one time or another, came down to visit.

There were bitter power-struggles with brain-cells of greater tenure or higher category than his own, but Skrov-Rogov had a good grounding in bureaucratic infighting, and he managed to keep control of his agency. With the Citizen Successor-Controller solidly behind him, he had his own brain-cell category revised upward twice, getting a special waiver of time-in-category from the Committee on Grants and Waivers. This was deemed necessary, not only for his own status, but so that he might have authority over the high-category specialists that were assigned to his agency.

He contrived that everything learned from the Outsiders must pass over his desk, that the different specialists were kept in ignorance of the details of each other's work, and that the extent to which Vandro Hannaro and the other aliens participated in the work was kept to a minimum. The Outsiders were, to the greatest extent possible, to be amused rather than informed; and they were to teach rather than be taught.

He also made sure that the area was surrounded by a high fence, and kept under constant guard. Whenever any of the Outsiders left it, they were always attended by members of the Organic State Police—to protect them from embarrassment and annoyance, he explained, because there was considerable fear of them and resentment of them among the more ignorant people. This, of course, would pass away in time; but for the present—

The only trouble with this explanation was that the Outsiders refused to understand. The concept of the ignorant public was one Skrov-Rogov was weaned on: the body-cells, the working mass, the serfs. But the Outsiders persisted in thinking he was referring to feeble-minded or organically brain-damaged people, and wondering why they were allowed to roam around. Won't they hurt themselves? And this problem did not lessen as time passed. It almost seemed as if, as communication between the races improved, mutual incomprehension increased.

Skrov-Rogov almost collided with Harv-Sarov, a priest and professor at the Sacred University of Urava, as he emerged from the main doorway of the Outsiders' Guest House. They snarled angrily at one another, and then, as mutual recognition dawned, apologized, laughing ruefully.

"It's no wonder that our tempers are short, Citizen," Harv-Sarov said. "The wonder is that we aren't biting one another. Dealing with those animals is surely a case of Vran testing our patience, our faith, and our fortitude. They are lying to us, those Outsider animals, and laughing in our faces, and we have to smile and pretend to believe them."

"You think so, Citizen?" Skrov-Rogov asked, taking the priest's arm and guiding him to a nearby bench. "I wish I could believe that."

Harv-Sarov looked at him in surprise. "Explain, Citizen Skrov-Rogov."

"Look at it this way, Citizen Priest-Professor; if they're lying, they must have a reason for lying, and we should be able to figure out what it is. If they're not lying, if they're telling the truth, it would invalidate everything we have been taught to believe in all our lives. It's like one of those problems in truth-telling you get in school: 'three people are locked in a room; one of them can only lie, one can either lie or tell the truth, and the third can only tell the truth. What question can you ask any one of them to instantly know which he is, and which the other two are?' Well, in real life the problem is invalid, because nobody always lies or always tells the truth. But with these Outsiders, we are faced with just that problem."

"How do you mean, Citizen?"

"Let me put it this way, Reverend Citizen; these beings claim not to understand what we're talking about when we tell them about the Organic State, because they don't have such a thing. Well, that's all right. There was a time when we had not evolved to the high point we're now at. So what sort of government do they have? We haven't been able to find out. Why? Because they have no word for the very concept of 'government.' They don't know what we're talking about."

The priest nodded. "Their language, if we are to believe what they tell us, lacks terms for the fundamental social relationships of authority, or regulation, or even law."

"And yet," Skrov-Rogov said, gesturing toward the landing field, from which one of the shuttles was thrusting itself into the atmosphere, climbing its ladder of flame, "they have developed a culture which has produced that. What sort of culture had we before the Citizen-Originator Dov-Soglov and the Citizen-First-Controller Zov-Zolkov? Guns that loaded at the muzzle with loose powder; wretchedly inefficient steam-turbines; no telephones or radio or electric power. Why, all that we have accomplished was accomplished under the Organic State, and yet these creatures, far in advance of our science, claim that they have no equivalent to the Organic State. Worse; they claim they possess no equivalent to the state! Their condition, they would have us think, is more anarchic than any in recorded history." He used an oath at which the priest frowned. "Can we believe them? And, more to the point, Citizen-Priest, *dare* we believe them?"

Harv-Sarov tied his two hands together with his fingers and stared glumly at the rough concrete walk. "I see what you mean, Citizen Director. But their problem goes much deeper for one of the Shoe, like myself. Their pretended ignorance of the very concepts of religion strike me to my soul. What are we to do with a race like this? How can they have achieved a high state of civilization, and not come to any awareness of the Glory of Vran?

How would He have permitted such a thing? Could it be that He is testing us?"

"Would that not be a reassuring answer, Reverend Citizen?"

"For you, perhaps, but not for me. If we are being tested by Vran, then what are the right answers to the test? What is it that Vran would have us do?" He turned to Skrov-Rogov and spread his hands wide, a gesture of bafflement. "Why, the most degraded savage in the darkest corner of the globe before the Englightenment had some concept, dim and barbarous though it might have been, of Vran. Yet you should have heard that female Outsider, the one called Leel-lah Something-Or-Other, with the bright red fuzz on her body and the white splash under her chin. She laughed at me when I tried to explain the existence of the Universe in the Mind of Vran. I tell you, I could hear that laugh echoing in the convolutions of the Mind itself. You know what she asked me? She asked me to tell her whose mind Vran existed in!"

"I saw a peasant on Vashtur hanged by the wrists over a slow fire and roasted to death for such blasphemous talk," Skrov-Rogov said.

"May he find forgiveness in the Memory of Vran," the priest mumbled, making the Holy Sign. "But that's not the worst of it. Disbelief we can handle, even from aliens. The Successor-Controller has authorized the Office of the Stabilization of the Faith to start a new Bench. It will be called the Bench for the Propagation of the Word of Vran Among the Outsiders. Of course, we are not to do any propagating now; nothing to annoy the fuzzy

beasts yet. But when we have the upper hand—
we'll convert them, or we'll eliminate the race
trying!"

"That's the idea," Skrov-Rogov approved.

"But their attitude, and their behavior; I don't
know how long I can stand it. They have no sense
of shame or morality. They degrade women by let-
ting them do men's work."

"They do seem to have complete equality of the
sexes," Skrov-Rogov said.

"Disgusting!" the priest said. "And have you
seen how they behave toward each other? Running
around naked; both sexes bathing together. And
they certainly like to bathe—they're the cleanest
beasts I ever saw. And the other day I came across
two of them under a tree—a male and a female.
And they were—openly—fornicating. And when
they saw me watching, it didn't seem to bother
them at all. Not at all. Just like animals."

"And yet—" Skrov-Rogov looked toward the
landing field. "The problem is real. If they're lying
to us—in word, deed, and behavior—they are not
only impeccably schooled in the lie, but they must
have a powerful motive. What could it be? And if
they are not lying, if their every word and every
action reflects what they truly believe, who they
truly are—" He paused, thoughtfully. "Why?" he
asked, of the air in front of him, not of the priest.
"Why would the universe look thus to them and
thus to us? And who is right?"

"Citizen Skrov-Rogov!" the priest said, the
shock evident in his voice.

Yssa Balkadranna looked up from the writing-machine and her stack of notes as Lylla Rovorrido came into the room and laid her notebook on the table in front of Vandro.

"Anything new?" Vandro asked.

Lylla shrugged. "I'm afraid I horrified one of them, again. Harv-Sarov, the one who always wears that blue smock with the gold trimmings, and the shoes with the gold buckles. Just asked him a simple question, too. These people are so sensitive, and about the silliest things."

Dantro Fanzagarro, who had been dozing on a couch across the room, opened one eye. "What was it this time, Lylla?" he asked. "Tizzy and Puzzy and Vran; or the mind-cells and the body-cells and everybody in his place?"

"It was Tizzy and Puzzy this time. It seems you mustn't ask questions about that. What kind of a civilization can you develop if you can't ask questions? How did they get as advanced as they are without asking questions? And how did they ever get a system of beliefs like that?"

"Don't ask me," Dantro said. "Ask them."

"I have done so," Lylla said. "I asked why I shouldn't ask, and he told me not to ask that. And I then asked him how we could learn if we didn't ask."

"What did he say to that?" Vandro asked.

"He said I was only to ask the approved questions, that that was the only way to learn."

Yssa leaned back in her chair and stretched her arms over her head. "I hate to say this," she said, "but I'm beginning to suspect that Our Sister's Children are crazy. All of them."

"Yssa," Vandro said, looking up from the

notebook, "that's not fair, really. Different from us, even very different, is not necessarily crazy."

"I don't mean different from us," Yssa said. "I mean crazy. Not sane."

"The whole planet? All the people?"

"If this is a representative sample, yes. Of course there's always the possibility that we've landed in an insane asylum. I spent some time working in an insane asylum in my youth. There are certain similarities in behavior between the poor unfortunates in there, and the people of this planet."

"Well, they don't run around frothing at the mouth and biting people, and they don't go off and sit in dark corners with blankets over their heads, mumbling to themselves. That's how all the crazy people I've ever seen acted," Vandro said.

"You never saw that poor woman at Salgrazzo's Town, did you?" Lylla asked. "The one whose child burned to death in the grainery fire? She refuses to believe the child is dead, and goes all around town hunting for it and calling its name. She isn't sane, is she?"

"Thank you, Lylla," Yssa said. "That's the sort of thing I mean. I think we have a whole planet here that suffers from what that poor woman suffers from. It's a systematic rejection of reality and substitution of delusion-belief. That woman couldn't endure the reality of her baby's death, and so she rejected it. She substituted the fiction that the child was alive somewhere out of her sight. No one can convince her of the truth; for her, the delusion has *become* the truth."

"So?" Vandro asked. "I sympathize with the poor woman, but what has that to do with Our Sister's Children?"

"That woman and these people have the same sort of non-sanity. Sanity, in this context, consists of thinking-patterns that are in agreement with perceptible reality. What that woman did, and what these people are doing, is rejecting reality and setting up a consistent system of delusion-beliefs."

"But that woman was under a tremendous stress," Vandro said. "You can't think every person on this planet has had a loved-one burn to death?"

"That woman," Yssa said, "was under a tremendous stress for a very short period of time. What would happen to someone who was put under a smaller stress, but over a much longer period of time?"

"I don't know," Vandro said.

"Neither do I," Yssa admitted, "but I think there's a pretty good chance that it's the explanation of what's happened here."

Dantro swung his legs over the edge of the couch and sat up. "Now, there's an idea we want to kick around for a while," he said. "I'm glad it occurred to Yssa, for it wouldn't have occurred to any of the rest of us. We don't have many really non-sane people at home; and those we have are cared for out of common funds in special asylums. We've never found any way to cure these people, although sometimes they get well spontaneously. Is that right, Yssa?"

"That's right," she said.

"So," Dantro continued, "we don't understand deviations from sanity too well. Most of us tend to think of frothing at the mouth, or other obvious symptoms. But you can't tell that delusional people are crazy; not unless you happen to know the truth about whatever their delusion is. I mean, if you were a stranger in Salgrazzo's Town, and ran across that poor woman, you'd have no reason to think she wasn't looking for a perfectly real, living child, that just happened to be out of sight.''

"That's true," Vandro agreed. "So, what's the point?"

"The point is that if these people are really non-sane, we'll have to stop trying to deal with them as though they were sane. It won't do any good."

"Maybe it's just a question of different kinds of sanity," Vandro suggested.

"Oh, no!" Dantro expostulated. "Didn't we just define sanity as thinking in a manner in agreement with objective reality? How many kinds of reality are there, anyhow? I mean, it's not insane to believe that your child is missing if you have no evidence to the contrary. But if you have perfectly objective evidence that your child is dead, such as having seen the body, then continuing to believe that it is merely missing, while unfortunate and pathetic, is also insane.''

"Well, while we're on the subject, how about this Tizzy-Puzzy-Vran business?" Lylla asked. "Is that sanity, now? We have a universe which we know—not just assume; know from actual physical-structure examination—to be composed of quanta of energy, grouped into atoms, which are grouped into molecules, which are grouped into macroscopic masses. Yssa, you're the physicist; do we or don't we know that?''

"Well—" Yssa looked up at the ceiling, wrinkling the fur between her eyes. "When I perform an experiment, and check the results with my senses, and check my senses against one another and against instruments, and somebody else performs the same experiment and our results agree; and then another researcher uses those results to set up a second-stage experiment and predicts the results accurately based on our data . . . Yes, without getting onto any ontological-epistemological merry-go-round, I'd say we know that."

"All right. Now then, what about this universe-in-the-Mind-of-Vran? Without cracking wise about what would happen if Vran ever got seriously absent-minded, I say that the whole thing is systematized delusion and rejection of reality; and if that isn't a description of non-sanity, I'd like to hear one. The very fact that they won't allow themselves to ask questions ought to be proof enough. You try to convince that woman we were talking about that her child isn't alive, and see what happens."

"That's the sort of thing I mean," Yssa said. "But what I was thinking about, more than Tizzy and Puzzy, was this big animal that they all think they're parts of. Now, if that's an example of sanity, then I'll kiss the man who calls me crazy!"

"But, Yssa," Vandro objected, "they don't really believe that they're cells in the body of some big animal. That's just a sort of figure of speech. They mean that they have constituted their society so that it resembles a living organism—"

"I know perfectly well what they mean. They mean that a little gang that call themselves the brain-cells can tell everybody else what to do and what not to do, and what to wear and eat, and who to mate with, and where to work, and what house to live in; and everybody thinks it's for their own good, and it's the way Vran intended for them to live. And if you don't happen to think so, why then you're too afraid to mention it to anyone. You know what would happen at home if anybody tried any trash like that? You know how long the Halzorro Gang lasted, after they tried to do about one-millionth of what this Organic State thing gets away with? Why, as nearly as I can see, the whole and sole purpose of this Organic State thing is to make everybody as wretched as possible. Beside that, the Tizzy-Puzzy-Vran thing is practically sane. You know what I think? I think we ought to go home, all of us, and blow up the ship, and dismantle the radio station on Skystabber, and forget all about this place. The way these beings behave isn't just non-sane; it's *anti*-sane!"

Chapter Fourteen

As he sat by the window just forward of the edge of the plane's wing, waiting for Valla Alvararro to get the transport into the air, Vandro Hannaro thought, for the thousandth time, of what Yssa had said twenty years before, and found himself wishing devoutedly that her advice had been followed. When it came to that, he wished that his mother had interested herself in anything besides contacting Shining Sister, that he had found his mother's interests boring, that Kartho Alvararro had broken his neck halfway up Skystabber. But it was too late, now, even for regrets. The destinies of the twin planets were inextricably tangled, and could only get more so.

The plane shuddered slightly as Valla fed more fuel into her jets to keep them hot. Opening his eyes, Vandro saw that they were still motionless in the same place.

"Valla!" he called. "What's the delay?"

"It's the plane ahead of us," she replied. "A big Zemnovarro Gang transport. It should be taxi-ing over to the edge of the runway for the take-off run, but the Zemnovarro's are having some kind of a hassle with some passengers. They look like greenies. Probably claiming that their luggage has been searched, judging by my experience with the breed."

Vandro twisted in his seat and looked forward along the direction his plane was pointing. The big six-jet transport ahead of them was in the next slot for the runway, but instead of the gangway stairs being pulled away, there were fifteen green-skinned, green-downed natives of Shining Sister gathered around the foot of the gangway. While the transport rumbled in place, alternately puffing its jets, two of the green-skins were gesticulating angrily as they argued with a couple of members of the Zemnovarro Gang, while the rest stood in a clump. Only three of them were armed; they would be members of the Organic State Police, each watching the other two while all of them watched the rest.

This was typical of relations between the two planets and their races. He remembered the first of Shining Sister's Children to visit his world. There had been twelve, including Skrov-Rogov. He and two others, members of the Organic State Police, had brought weapons, the peculiarly-shaped automatics designed for a two-thumbed hand, and had gone to considerable trouble to secrete them. They probably thought they were succeeding, too, despite the tell-tale bulges in their clothing, until one of their guides asked them why the others were not also armed. None of them would go anywhere or do anything without the permission of Skrov-Rogov. None of them would talk to any Hetairan alone. As a result, they did everything in a clump.

They were given a tremendous ovation everywhere they went, and taken to see everything of interest. They would go to tremendous lengths to learn, in strange, sneaky ways, all sorts of things that they could have found out simply by asking. When they were about to go back, one of their pieces of luggage had broken open and it was revealed stuffed with notes and books of all sorts of scientific and technical information. They went into a panic of discovery, which amazed the Hetairans, who, in turn tried to convince them that they didn't care; that the Thalassans were free to take back whatever they wished. Which amazed the Thalassans even more.

"They're always screaming that we're searching their luggage," the girl sitting beside Vandro said. "They never have gotten it inside their heads that we don't care where they come or go, or what they take—as long as they pay for it."

"Maybe it would be a good idea to search their luggage occasionally," Vandro said. "We'd find out what they're so afraid of, and give more of an air of reality to their fears."

"That's the lot from Zagannos' Landing," another of his companions said. "Four of them wouldn't go back; said they'd rather stay on a decent world and dig ditches for a living. So the Zagannos took them in, of course. That's what the rest are so sore about."

That had started early in the course of interplanetary relations, too. A member of the second group of visitors from Shining Sister had eluded the Organic State Police guards and taken refuge with a lumbering gang in the mountains.

When his absence was discovered, the others had demanded the right to go back and get him. They were amazed when they were told that they were free to go wherever they liked, including back after their wandering planet-mate. They were never able to quite believe that, and always behaved as though they thought it was some kind of trap. And then when they went back to the lumbering gang and demanded their man, they were turned away at rifle point. Krav-Torov himself demanded the fugitive's return, and was quite incredulous when informed that, if he couldn't get him out, then nobody else could.

By this time the attitude of the Organic State was becoming more understandable. Krav-Torov and his government feared that contact with the Hetairans would spread dissatisfaction with the Organic State and doubt of the Puzzán Creed among his people. Sanity, it would appear, was a dangerously contagious disease. The whole situation, and the behavior of Krav-Torov, became most understandable when viewed by analogy to the quarantines established by the ranching gangs of the plains during the recurring cattle-plagues.

Trade, of course, was difficult under such circumstances. On Thalassa, only the Organic State was allowed to buy or sell, or even own, commodities in bulk. And the Organic State had to be watched with two unblinking eyes if you were going to deal with it. Every grain of cereal had to be counted, every bag of produce weighed and smelled before it could be accepted. Business ethics, it seemed, were not a part of the Organic State.

For a long time Krav-Torov believed, in spite of

repeated denials and extensive explanations, that the Shining Sister Combine was a government like his own. It was not until the Zaganno Gang built a space-ship of their own and began trading in direct competition with the Shining Sister Combine that he learned otherwise.

Then he got the bright idea of having his agents try to foment trouble between the Zagannos and the Combine, but they couldn't seem to get a handle on it. The charges that they whispered in appropriate ears were so ridiculous that, instead of believing them, one gang would call the other to chortle, "Say, what do you suppose a green-skin told me you boys were up to today?"

Then the agents of the Organic State got the bright idea of trying to break the Trading Combine with floods of counterfeit trade certificates. Those who were caught at it were summarily shot, which did nothing to improve interplanetary feelings. The ether was hot for a while with radio-beamed threats of reprisal and counter-reprisal. Both sides were bluffing, the one because they didn't dare start anything, and the other because there was no sort of supra-gang government to do any reprising if they had wanted to. Of course, any gang or combine would have been free to take on the Organic State all by itself.

By then, thanks to the almost ineradicable Hetairan belief that scientific information should be freely shared and exchanged, the Thalassans had nuclear power-reactors all over their planet, buying uranium and plutonium from Hetaira. Within a short time after this, they had built a space-ship of their own.

The Zaganno Gang, unable to compete profit-
ably with the Shining Sister Combine, sent their
ship on a voyage of exploration to the tiny first
planet of the system. It was airless, blazingly hot on
the hemisphere facing the sun, and space-cold on
the far side; but there was a narrow twilight-ribbon
where, if they were canny, they could put their air-
locked dome in the shade and extend low-pressure
heat collectors into the sunlight for warmth and
power. They were able to find oxygen, carbon diox-
ide, and water locked in the rocks of the far side,
and in a pocket in the twilight zone they found
fabulously rich deposits of pitchblende and
uranite.

By this time the first emotional love for Shining
Sister's Children had evaporated, and along with it
the willingness to share information. The Zaganno
Gang kept their operations on the First Planet a
secret for a very long time.

Vandro felt the plane vibrating under him as it
moved into position for the take-off run. The Zemnovarro transport was already airborne; the Zem-
novarros had probably given the grass-heads the
choice of getting on or being left behind.

"The Zagannos probably caught that bunch
snooping, and booted them out," the girl said.
"Which, in my opinion, was a dumb trick. What
they should have done was shot the lot of them!"

"And give the grass-heads an excuse to massacre
our people on Shining Sister?" another of the party
asked.

"They wouldn't dare do that; we have four
space-ships to their one, and they know it. We'd
have all four of them over there launching their

shuttles and dumping explosives down on them before one of their missionaries could recite ten stanzas from That Book!"

The missionaries had been one of Krav-Torov's bigger mistakes. They had come over in groups, two-by-two, to convert the heathen Outsiders, bringing with them thousands of copies of The Books of Tissé to be distributed freely among the furry people. Well, the furry people took the books; they had an innate love of books of any description. They also listened to the missionaries. But, try as they would, the missionaries made no converts. None.

What it took Krav-Torov almost two years to figure out was that the people of the Horizon Object thought the missionaries were funny. When he realized this, he decided to make the best use of the missionaries he could. The problem of converting the heathens was put to one side, and the missionaries were converted into spies. They were not very effective spies. The Hetairans had no secrets, a fact that Krav-Torov never understood, but they did believe in safeguarding their possessions. So, when missionaries were found snooping around in places they shouldn't be, they were shot. Just like anyone else would have been.

Which, of course, convinced Krag-Torov that the Outsiders did, indeed, have secrets. So he sent more missionaries. Pretty soon the Hetairans longer thought they were funny.

Vandro turned to the girl at his side. "I hope it doesn't come to that, Janna," he said. "But it looks like it will eventually come to something. We can't put up with their slimy tricks forever. Maybe if we gave them a good banging around, we might knock some civilized manners into them."

Thirty years after the coming of the Outsiders, Skrov-Rogov sat in the chair that had been Krav-Torov's before him, and Tov-Varsov's, and Rav-Razkov's, and Zov-Zolkov's at Karkasha. He had played well the cards Vran had dealt him. His liaison agency had, after his return from the first trip to the Horizon Object, become a full Control Bureau, with himself elevated to first brain-cell category and placed at its head; and, because of the paramount importance of the Horizon Object and its strange, fuzzy people in the affairs of the Organic State, he had come to stand second only to the Successor-Controller in the councils of the State. When Krav-Torov died, it had been only natural for him to be elected to the Successor-Controllership.

"Why didn't they attack us at the very beginning?" Nov-Borsov, the Deputy-Controller of the Armed Forces, wondered. "That's what I should have done in their place. And why did they let us learn so much from them? After all these years we still can't understand the way they think. It's unreasonable!"

"It was the Will of Vran," Harv-Sarov, the Dean of Archpriests, declared. "Vran was testing us with these Outsiders, but Vran would not suffer His people to be overwhelmed by the infidel."

The others looked at him in deprecation. That sort of talk was all right to give to the body-cells and the lower category brain-cells, but entirely out of place at a meeting of the First Category.

"How could those anarchists, with no internal organization and nobody in command, ever hope to coordinate their forces well enough to wage a successful war of conquest against the Organic State?" Morv-Gorov, the Deputy Controller of Security, demanded scornfully.

"They could have. You should know that, Citizen. With their weapons, it would have taken very little organization to have defeated us utterly," Skrov-Rogov said. Had anyone else uttered those words, it could have been considered treason. "But they were too crafty. They had other weapons with which to subdue us. They could, and did, make us dependent upon them for power-metals. They could, and did, make us dependent upon them for technological goods that we are incapable of making. And they could, and I regret to say that in the cases of some of the weak and degenerate among us, they did, corrupt us."

"Yes!" The Dean of Archpriests nodded and slapped his hand sharply down on the conference table. "Their abominable atheism; their lawless and anarchic way of life; their beastly immorality and lack of shame!"

"And now we find out," the Successor-Controller said, "that they have seized the First Planet, and planted a colony there. This colony is where their steady supply of the power-metals is coming from. And when, quite by accident, one of our spies finds this out, and we demand a just share of these interplanetary riches—which, by rights, should belong to everybody equally—they refuse us utterly."

"They laugh at us," Morv-Grov put in, angrily.

"And, with the exception of insignificant deposits of low-grade fissionable ores on Thurv, we are without any uranium whatever that we do not buy from them." The Successor-Controller shifted in his chair. "This is an intolerable position for the Organic State, and one which we are no longer prepared to bear. Nov-Borsov?"

The Deputy-Controller of the Armed Forces rose. "Two new-model space-ships are ready," he said. "Secretly built over the past two years; these are fighting ships, armed with rocket-bombs, and carrying two hundred and eighty-eight fighting men each. These men have been equipped with space-suits, and trained to fight on a low-gravity, airless world."

"How were they trained?" asked the Deputy-Controller of Agriculture.

"In special large tanks, under water," Nov-Borsov replied. "Our experts have concluded that such an environment closely approximates conditions on the surface of the First Planet."

"They will depart shortly from the side of the planet out of sight of the Horizon Object," Skrov-Rogov said. "It will take some six hundred hours for them to reach the First Planet. Our agents have located the mining colony to within a few hundred leagues, so there should be no trouble finding the domes on the surface. Our fighters should have little trouble overwhelming the colony."

"It is the Will of Vran," the Dean of Archpriests said firmly.

Errba Zaganno, defensive screen observer for the Third Shift Watch, observed the two little blips on the radar screens as two mysterious ships rounded the curve of the First Planet, headed toward the Zaganno mining colony. They were not coming in from the right direction for Zaganno ships, they did not show the automatic identification code of Zaganno ships, and there were no Zaganno ships expected. She hit the general alarm button, and flipped the missile delivery radar onto automatic tracking. "Visitors!" she yelled.

The head of the communications section, Dandro Zaganno, came running into the screen room from the general mess, a soup spoon still forgotten in his hand. "What have you got?"

"I think they're unfriendlies," Errba said. "I'm trying the spaceship general-hailing frequencies now, and they don't respond."

"What are they aiming for?" Dandro asked, glaring into the screen.

Errba flicked a couple of switches and tapped a tune into the small keyboard below the screen complex. A dotted line appeared on the big screen, predicting where the objects would go with no further rocket burn.

"They're coming in low, directly over our heads," she said.

Dandro stared at the screen for a few more seconds, and then shook his head. "Any gang would know better than that," he said. "They're greenies, and they mean us no good. Blast them."

Errba Zaganno rotated a guard free of a large black button labeled LAUNCH, which had a row of twenty switches under it. She flipped the first and second switches up, and then pushed the button.

* * *

"Don't look at me like that!" Nov-Borsov barked, glaring defensively around the table. "My spacemen died fighting heroically against a cowardly ambush! They must have the whole terminator-zone of the First Planet honeycombed with launching sites. Our intelligence was faulty." He glanced sidewise at Morv-Gorov. "How does it happen that we didn't know about their missiles in advance—or even that the Outsiders had fission-bombs? What kind of espionage are those missionaries accomplishing anyway?"

"And how soon is it going to be before their ships are in orbit off this planet, launching fission-bombs into our cities?" somebody else demanded. "We all know how little fission-fuel we have available; they must have five bombs for every one we could build."

Skrov-Rogov held up a hand. "Citizens!" he reproved. "These recriminations are unbecoming to our dignity; they are useless as well. No one is at fault. If any were, you may all be sure that Organic Justice would have been done before this. The purpose of this meeting is to decide future actions, not to cry about the past. We were surprised, that's all. We lost two ships and many good body-cells. They can be replaced. Our situation is far from hopeless, despite our lack of adequate fissionable material. Citizen Tav-Jarov, it is now time to reveal the details of your secret project. Speak, and receive the thanks of the Organic State for what you have done."

"Inspired by the Will of Vran, and by the patterns of correct thinking imbued by the words of the departed Dov-Soglov, Citizen Successor-Controller," Jav-Tarov, the Deputy Controller of Scientific Advancement and Display, added, rising to his feet.

"Well, Citizens, I assume that everyone around this table knows enough of the principles of the Fission-bomb that I need not go into that. If I am wrong, see me after the meeting and I will recommend some rudimentary reading. You also know that, despite the exaggerated idea of some of our lower-category brain-cells, the amount of fissionable material on this planet is quite limited. Even by stripping our existing fission-power plants of their fuel to make bombs, an action that would be undesirable anyway, we would not be able to create sufficient fission weapons to decisively defeat and conquer the Horizon Object. And we dare not contemplate any war that falls short of immediate and decisive defeat.

"However, we have developed a radically new type of nuclear weapon. Instead of releasing energy by the chain-reaction of fissionable heavy nuclei, such as those of uranium or plutonium, we have found that an even greater energy release can be gained by the *fusion* of light nuclei, such as those of hydrogen or lithium. The ideal substance in which to produce such an energy-release is a combination of the two; lithium hydride. Weight for weight, fusion of lithium hydride will release three times the energy released by the fission of plutonium. Furthermore, the size of such a bomb will not be limited by any critical-mass factor; tons of lithium hydride can be packed around the small fission bomb which is necessary to furnish the intense heat to initiate the fusion reaction."

"Thank you, Citizen Tav-Jarov," Skrov-Rogov said. "You and your scientists have done well, and will be rewarded." He turned to the table. "Our rocket technicians assure me that it will be quite possible to build remote-controlled space rockets which can deliver, on the Horizon Object, bombs several thousand times more destructive than the conventional fission bomb. It is well within the power of the Organic State to create enough such rockets, with the fusion warheads devised by Tav-Jarov, to totally depopulate the Horizon Object. Furthermore, the lingering radiation will be of extremely short duration. In a matter of several years we will be able to go there and find a world, intact, but burned clean of the vile life which now infests it."

"And how long is it estimated that it will take to build this quantity of remote-controlled rockets and fusion bombs?" somebody asked.

"The rockets are the responsibility of Citizen Shev-Yorov's Bureau," Skrov-Rogov said. "He will be given everything he needs. Citizen Tav-Jorov assures me that his Bureau will be able to produce the actual bombs in three years at the most. Isn't that right?"

Tav-Jorov nodded. "That is so, Citizen Successor-Controller," he said.

Skrov-Rogov stood up. "Then we will proceed with this plan," he said. "The Horizon Object must be wiped clean! But all of you keep in mind that, until the moment comes, we must do everything to avoid open conflict with the Outsiders."

* * *

Vandro Hannaro, grimly sad, looked down the long table. Everybody who would be taking part in the conference was seated: the whole board of advisers of Shining Sister Combine, the leading advisers of the Trading Combine, the Board of the Banking Combine, the big industrial and ranching and agricultural combines, the Rendezvous Combine. Less than a hundred men and women were gathered here, and they were prepared to speak for the entire world. This was a moment unique in the history of his people, and Vandro Hannaro didn't like it. What was worse, any decision reached around this table would affect every gang and individual on the planet. The thing that a few conservatives had feared back when the Trading Combine was formed, three centuries before, was now coming to pass.

"Well, that's the situation," Arvo Zaganno, the spokesman for his gang, told the group. "We beat off the first attack on our mining outpost quite easily; probably because they didn't expect any resistance. They certainly weren't prepared to face remote-control rockets with nuclear warheads. But they'll be back; and we won't be able to face another attack alone. We can't put a radar screen around the whole planet; and we can't site missile launchers every twenty kilolances in every direction. They could land an army on the planet, once they build enough space-suits, and deploy and attack from several directions. Nuclear rockets designed to take out space ships aren't much use against a ground army, especially on an airless planet. We need your help to form a Grand Combine, and we believe it's in your interest."

"How does this affect us?" one of the Trading Combine demanded.

"If the grass-heads get onto the First Planet," Arvo said, "the fissionables monopoly is smashed. If *they* control the planet, *they* won't sell *us* any fissionables. They'll just build weapons with the surplus from their power-stations. And when they have enough nuclear weapons—does anyone want to guess what they'll do with them?"

"That might be a bit alarmist," one of the Banking Combine people said. "But he's right about the rest of it. All the fissionable ore on Shining Sister comes from those low-grade uranite mines on Thurv. If they get a foothold on the First Planet, we can close the books on any trade with them."

"Would that be such a bad thing?" an elderly representative of the Rendezvous Combine asked. "It seems to me, judging from past experiences, that we'd be better off without any dealings with them."

"Don't fool yourself, Zalgo," a woman from the Trading Combine said. "We'd have dealings with them—a kind we wouldn't like. If they get hold of the fissionables on the First Planet, they'd be invading us inside of ten years. I'm absolutely sure of that."

"Oh, rubbish, Nalla! They have a planet of their own—"

"With one-tenth our land-surface and ten times our population. This lovely planet of ours is just right to siphon off their surplus population to. And you don't know those snakes the way I do, Zalgo. When we make a deal, we try to come out even; everybody happy. They can't do that, can't stand the thought of it. They can't be even with anyone, they have to dominate. And, since they've brought their own world under a single tyranny, we're all they have left to conquer."

"Why? Why would they do that? Why would anyone want to—control—anybody else?"

"Some of them seem to thrive on controlling other people; it's a kind of sickness, I suppose. As for the others, it is their duty to Vran and the Organic State."

"That's what I've been trying to get across for the past thirty years," Yssa Balkadranna said. She was an old woman now, almost as old as Vandro himself; her dark red fur was beginning to assume the uniform whitish surface tinge of age, and her voice was sharp and petulant. "They're all crazy, every last one of them. And the ones who run the Organic State are the craziest of all. They hate and fear us; they can't even conceive that we came to them in love and friendship thirty years ago. Since they want so badly to dominate us, they have to believe that we want to dominate them. If we don't do something to stop them, they will be here; with guns and bombs and armored trucks, and all the weapons they can build with all the technology they learned from us!"

"Yes," Nalla took up the argument. "And if they get a foot-hold on the First Planet, they'll have all the fissionables they need; they can start building an invasion fleet and stockpiling fission bombs. This idea of a Grand Combine is all right as far as it goes, but it doesn't go far enough. We need a *World* Combine; with every gang in the world in it, to build a big enough space-fleet to pro-

tect both this and the First Planet against any attack. If we cut off trade with them, they'll attack
us. Maybe not at once, but sooner or later, and I'd
bet on sooner. They have plenty of fissionables
now, that we were fools enough to sell them."

Yssa stood up silently, and waited until the
cross-talk had died away, and everyone had turned
to look at her. "We can do better than that," she
said, clearly and firmly. "We can solve their population problem for them, by a one-hundred percent
reduction—and then we can stop worrying about a
raid on the First Planet, or an attack on us here.
And, I tell you, it's the only way to prevent them
from attacking us, as Nalla says, sooner or later."

"That would take quite a little doing, Yssa,"
Vandro said.

"Not too much. We can bombard their planet
with radio-guided rockets from here," she said.
"And we can case the bombs in cobalt."

"Cobalt? What would that do?" Zalgo asked.

"The energy-release of an ordinary fission-bomb
would be enough to convert a cobalt casing—of ordinary cobalt-58—into radioactive cobalt-60.
That's a gamma-emitter, with a five-year half-life.
A thousand or so of them would drench that planet
with lingering radiation for the next five centuries;
the whole planet would be literally sterilized, as far
as any air-breathing life was concerned. And that
would be the end of Tizzy-Puzzy and the Organic
State, and lying and cheating and trying to
Halzorro the whole planet; and we could go back
to living like civilized people."

There was a stir about the table; everybody, even
the Zaganno representatives, looked at her aghast.

"You're not serious about that, Yssa?" Vandro asked. Then he nodded. "Yes, you are."

"But if we were to do anything like that—could we go on as before?" Zalgo asked. "Bearing the guilt of a billion murders?"

"I suppose," Yssa said, sadly, "what I'm offering you is a choice of guilt. Doing this would not be easy; none of us would ever forget it. We would have to bear it with us all the rest of our lives. But, if we don't, what do we then have to live with? The knowledge that our children will surely be born into a world of fear and tyranny. Fear of the grass-heads, and tyranny of the World Combine we'll have to organize in self-protection. And the ever-present possibility that the grass-heads might break through whatever protective ring we form; and then our children would either be slaves or dead."

She looked slowly around the group. "There are very few of us here who haven't been forced, at one time or another, to kill somebody in self-defense, or defense of our property. None of us think of that as murder. Well, neither is this. It's a matter of our whole world defending itself against murderers and thieves and tyrants."

"But . . . after all, Yssa," the old man said, "they are Our Sister's Children."

"Tissé and Puzzá and Vran!" Yssa fairly screamed the obscenities. "After all these years, and all that's happened in them, are we still tangling ourselves in that silly metaphor? Our Sister's Vermin, you mean. Shining Sister has bugs in her fur. And I think we should scrub them out for her! And, speaking of that, there's an old saying: If you sleep with dirty people, you'll wake with your fur full of bugs. Well, look at what's crawling on us! Here we are talking about setting up a World Combine—eighty or ninety of us, making plans for everybody on the planet. And, since everybody never goes along with anything, no matter how good for them it's supposed to be, the plans will take coercion to carry out. The next thing, we'll be setting up orders and regulations, telling people what they must do, and what they can't do, and organizing a world-wide police gang to enforce our decisions. Why don't we just call it an organic state and be done with it?"

There was a long silence, while those about the table stared at each other. Then Yssa continued:

"Well, Citizen brain-cells? What do you see when you look at each other? What have these vermin of Shining Sister done to us even without attacking?"

"Yssa's right," Vandro said. "I'd sooner see our planet depopulated than see our children enslaved to a government. What an obscene concept this 'government' business is. When one person has power over another, he is corrupted by it. On Shining Sister both the power and the corruption are total. We must never let the filthiness of one person dominating another by some kind of hereditary bondage—called 'government'—come to this world. And the best—the only—way to prevent it is to sterilize the source of the infection."

Zalgo took a deep breath, and then nodded. "It's a decision that will be hard to live with," he said, "but it's the right decision. I vote for—sterilization."

Vandro turned to Yssa. "How long will it take to

produce the bombs, and the rockets to carry them."

Yssa sat down, suddenly looking very old and vulnerable. "About two years for the bombs," she said. "But, even if we start work at the same time on the rockets and launching sites, they'll take longer. I'd say about three years, total. Three years . . ."

Chapter Fifteen

Captain Absalom Carpenter consolidated some of his hand-written notes and spoke some more of his report into the expedition log, and then fixed himself another cold drink. From somewhere near at hand came the steady *chuck, chuck, chuck,* of machetes and the intermittent howl of a chain-saw as a working-party cleared the jungle away from the main entrance of the big temple, or palace, or whatever it was. The giant ruined structure was in better condition than anything else they'd found on the planet so far, and even it didn't look too promising.

"Man, this isn't anything!" Benedict Sokolov, the sociographer, declared, gulping a slug of rum and waving his cigar. He was short and fat, and aggressively unshaven and rumpled to advertise his civilian status. "Wait until you see Hetaira; that planet really got clobbered! There isn't a city, or even a really big town anywhere. But every place where a city or town ought to be, there's one of those great goddam big puddles of fused glass."

The captain nodded. "Most of the bombs that came down on this planet must have burst in the water. We've found surprisingly few craters on land. Of course, the Hetairans were using cobalt fission-bombs; a water burst would spread more radioactivity around, which must have been what they had in mind. There must have been some pretty impressive tidal waves; probably swept right across all but the biggest land-masses."

"What this crowd, here, used on Hetaira was thermonuclears," Kent Pickering, the physicist, said. He was slender and gray; and as foppishly neat and well-groomed as Sokolov was untidy. "Lithium-Hydrides; real king-size jobs. The fusion-mass of each one must have been on the order of four or five tons."

"I'll bet they made something to see, when they went off," Gert van Zyl, the biologist, said.

"From a long, long distance," Pickering told him. "I was on Beta Hydrae II when Carlos von Schlichten bombed Keegark; fact is, I was aboard the gun-cutter that dropped the bomb. To give you some sense of comparison, a round of pistol ammunition is to the Keegark bomb as the Keegark bomb is to one of the ones used on Hetaira. I haven't even tried to estimate the temperature at the center of one of those blasts, but the entire planet must have been swept by storms of incandescent gas, at from five hundred to a thousand degrees Centigrade."

"How does the isotope-decay dating compare with the dating here on Thalassa?" Carpenter asked.

"As we expected," Pickering said. "Some six hundred years, give or take ten percent. It's obvious that the rockets must have been launched simultaneously from both planets. The two flights must have passed each other in space. Neither planet would have had a chance to do anything more after they started landing. You know, that wasn't really a war. That was a suicide pact. Like a duel with submachine guns at two paces."

"These two peoples must have really loved each other," Carpenter said. He turned his attention to the biologist. "What's the life situation?" he asked. "I only glanced at your report; I got it a couple of hours ago."

"Well," van Zyle said, "there's a variety of in-vertebrate life in some of the larger bodies of water. And, surprisingly, we found quite a few insects. I should imagine their eggs are highly cold-resistant and were protected by having been frozen into deep ice, maybe hundreds or thousands of years before the blast. There is a wide variety of plant life, all deep-rooted perennials. At a hasty guess, I'd say that they had spread from no more than five or six places on the planet, which escaped the worst of the heat-storms by some fluke. And we found one form of mobile land-life—a nasty crawling thing like a ten-centimeter leech, in the mud flats around the small sea on the outside hemisphere. It seems to be the highest form of life on the planet. Has Ozukami made any progress on the first planet since I left?"

"Why, yes," Carpenter said, picking up his glass. "It's really quite extraordinary. It's been—what?—four days, and they can already communicate to some extent. Seem to be a really intelligent people. Look a lot like us—humanoid, I mean—but covered with fur. It was a mining colony from what we've called Hetaira. Been stranded there for six hundred years. They've been quite clever about surviving under those conditions, but they're slowly dying off. Probably lowered reproduction rates due to the natural radioactivity in the rocks they're surrounded by."

The Captain paused for another pull at his drink. "They have no real idea of what's happened here," he said. "They're out of sight of either planet. All they know for sure is that, six hundred years ago, their space-ships stopped coming. They surmise that there was an atomic war, and that their people's technological base was so knocked out that they could no longer build space-ships. They're wondering what's taking the re-building so long."

"How did they react when Ozukami told them?"

"He hasn't told them yet," Carpenter said. "They want to go home. How do you tell them that their home-planet is now a sheet of glass? Or that their nearest living relative is now a ten-centimeter leech?"

"I certainly don't know," van Zyle said. "I would say that's Zucker's job. He's the ship psychologist. Where is he?"

Carpenter indicated the sleeping-shelter behind him with his thumb. "In there," he said. "He's been drinking, which he is not used to, so I had to put him to bed. He doesn't know, either."

FRED SABERHAGEN

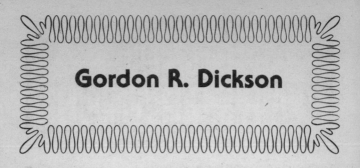

Gordon R. Dickson

□ 16015	Dorsai!	1.95
□ 34256	Home From The Shore	2.25
□ 56010	Naked To The Stars	1.95
□ 63160	On The Run	1.95
□ 68023	Pro	1.95
□ 77417	Soldier, Ask Not	1.95
□ 77765	The Space Swimmers	1.95
□ 77749	Spacial Deliver	1.95
□ 77803	The Spirit Of Dorsai	2.50

Available wherever paperbacks are sold or use this coupon.